MERCEDES
GENERAL

Also By Jerry L. Wheeler

Pangs

Strawberries & Other Erotic Fruit

MERCEDES GENERAL

STORIES BY
JERRY L. WHEELER

QUEERMOJO
A Rebel Satori Imprint
New Orleans & New York

Published in the United States of America by
Queer Mojo
A Rebel Satori Imprint
www.rebelsatoripress.com

"The Incident" was previously published in *Jonathan: A Journal of Queer Male Fiction*, edited by Raymond Luczak (Sibling Rivalry Press, 2014)

Paperback ISBN: 978-1-60864-299-1

ACKNOWLEDGEMENTS

I have learned my lesson. Never put the title of a project in your biography unless that project is finished. Every bio in every contest, book, or story I've been connected with bears a mention of *The Dead Book*. First, it's coming in 2011, then 2015, then 2017, and then the dates stop and it's just "forthcoming."

The Dead Book was not to be. Why? Lots of boring reasons. But the meat of that book was a series of flashbacks that eventually became the stories you're holding—*Mercedes General*, a collection of pieces about the deaths, both literal and figurative, in the lives of my two protagonists, Kent Mortenson and Spencer Michalek.

In the twenty years since the first story was written, I have a bunch of people to thank for reading them in various incarnations, including the original Denver Men's Writer's Group (Drew Wilson, Sean Wolfe, Matt Kailey, Peter Damien Clarke, and John Brandstetter), Jameson Currier, Raymond Luczak, Hank Edwards, 'Nathan Smith, Kevin Klehr, Tom Cardamone, and Joseph Campbell as well as my new writer's group, Write on the Hill (Vincent Meis, Eric Peterson, T.M. Tait, Bill Brown, Gayla Cook, Da'Shawn Mosley, Tyrone Umrani, and Rebecca Baldwin Fuller). Marshall Moore also deserves boatloads of thanks for his insights, advice, and friendship. Thanks also to Brian Alessandro for the kind words.

And, of course, thanks to Matt Bright at Inkspiral Design for the cover and Sven Davisson at Rebel Satori Press for his encouragement in helping make a twenty-plus year goal a reality. I am forever in their debt.

And a huge thanks to Rob Byrnes for the NYC info. Who else would you go to?

JW

CONTENTS

FRINGE

hat's the new kid," Suey whispered to me. We'd walked down the mountain to the bus stop on U.S. 40 after spending the night at Miss Lee's house. Mom needed *some time away from the kids.* She needed a lot of that, so it was lucky we lived in the little house across the lawn from Miss Lee. "His mom's a drunk," she added.

I wasn't sure what I was supposed to do with that information, but I nodded my head and pretended it made a difference to me. It definitely made one to Suey. She puffed herself up some, putting on that swagger she used when she was off to show Katrina and Bonnie a new Barbie, like the one with the wedding gown she got last week. I didn't like her then.

Come to think of it, I didn't like her, period. I had to carry that dumb purse with her Barbie clothes and shoes, wait for her to hand out the Oreos mom gave her to share with me, and watch stupid *Bonanza* instead of *Batman* (even though Michael Landon made my stomach feel funny). It was getting old. I was clearly an unwanted possession: a living, breathing doll she couldn't dress up or have pretend tea with but had to take care of anyway. Or else she'd have to face Mom, which neither of us wanted to do. Suey was braver and talked back more than I did, but mostly to Dad. Nobody crossed Mom. Except Miss Lee.

The closer we got to the new kid, the more she puffed up. She had a white-knuckle grip on the rolled-up top of her lunch sack. Her blonde eyebrows were angled in a frown over her mean, blue eyes. Her nose was wrinkled, and her tight mouth set in a determined line. I knew that look, and it wasn't good.

I noticed his eyes first. They were blue like hers, but I was amazed at how different blue eyes could be. His had laugh lines at the corners, and when he smiled, I saw one of his front teeth was chipped. He wore his brown hair long over his ears, the way Mom wouldn't let me wear mine. And she would never have bought me a fringed suede jacket like he had on, much less allowed me to wear jeans as faded as his. Mine were always new and stiff. And he was carrying a Beatles lunchbox instead of our old Gibson's paper sacks.

"Hey," he said, raising two fingers in a peace sign.

I started to do the same thing, but Suey pulled my arm down. "Mom says we're not supposed to talk to strangers."

"I'm not a stranger," he said. "I'm a kid. Hey, is the bus always late?"

"Yeah," I replied. "The driver's a goon." Without knowing why, but knowing he'd appreciate it, I made my goon face. He crossed his eyes and smiled, and my heart swelled in my chest.

"I'm Spencer." He held his hand out for me to shake, which surprised me. I thought he was way too cool to do something my dad and his friends did, but I shook it anyway.

"I'm Kent." He didn't ask Suey her name. He didn't look at

her, either. He kept staring at me and grinning. I grinned back. At least I think I did. "Cool jacket," I said.

"Thanks. You live in that big house up top of the mountain?"

I shook my head. "We live in the little one across from it. The big one belongs to Miss Lee. She's our grandmother."

She moved between us. "Don't tell him anything. He doesn't need to know where we live. He lives in the caretaker's cabin."

"She must be your big sister," he said, peeking around her.

"Yeah," I said. I loved to feel her simmering. Someone was paying attention to me for a change, not her. Almost like she wasn't there. Except she *was* there. And if I knew my sister at all, she was about to remind us of her presence.

She turned to him. 'Your mom's a *drunk*," she sneered.

I stepped around her, hoping he wasn't going to cry and praying he would so I could comfort him. But he wasn't crying. "No shit, Sherlock," he said. "Tell me something I don't know."

Suey stepped back as if he'd slapped her, but then she smiled. My blood just about ran cold. I hated it when she smiled. She was extra mean when she smiled. She pointed to his lunchbox.

"You like the Beatles, huh?" she asked. This was one of her favorite moves. Find some common ground with your enemy, then yank it out from beneath him once he steps on it. It always worked. If I said anything, she'd sock me. I didn't want him to see that.

"Yeah, I do."

"Who's your favorite one?"

"John. He's the smartest." He may have been talking to her, but he was still looking at me. Maybe he was trying to glean something about my sister's sudden interest in the Beatles, or maybe, just maybe, he was as fascinated by me as I was him.

"He's a *fag*," Suey said, "so you must be a fag too."

I had some idea of what that meant but couldn't suss the details out from anyone. I knew it was bad enough to start fights, though. Except Spencer didn't seem too bothered by it. Maybe he was a fag. The thought thrilled me, but I couldn't concentrate on it. He stared at her with a slight, contemptuous grin then looked slowly away, his eyes resting back on me.

He's not afraid of her.

Suey saw it too. Two of her best shots had failed to rattle him. As short and skinny as he was, he stood more immovable, more imperturbable than any enemy I'd seen her encounter before. He was suffused with an inner calm and, what's more, I felt that peacefulness when I looked into his eyes. They reached in and stroked my soul. I never wanted to look away. Maybe we could be fags together.

But Suey wasn't about to give up. She hadn't made her bones as a bully by backing down in the face of a little adversity, or even a little adversary. She stepped forward and flipped a lock of his hair. Like I wanted to do, but for different reasons. "Just like a little girl," she cooed. "Just like a queer."

He didn't flinch, and he didn't back away. But he did look up at her and speak with dead calm. "Don't touch me."

Suey had had about all the challenges she could endure. She pushed his shoulders hard with both hands, the crinkling sound of her lunch sack mingling with a grunt.

His jacket fringe flew. He fell backward but not down, grabbing hold of some tall weeds with his free hand while he steadied himself. He planted his feet solidly, then took off straight for Suey with his shoulder down as if to ram her. She spread her feet apart and hunched down waiting for it, but at the last second, Spencer hit the brakes and put all that momentum into the arm with the lunchpail, aiming it at the side of Suey's head.

He connected with a solid thud to her ear. She yelped, dropped her lunch, and clamped both hands over her ear as the bus pulled up and opened its doors with a whoosh.

"Don't mess with me," Spencer warned her from his perch on the treaded stairs of the bus. "*Ever.*"

He had won. He had taken her on and won—and if he could, I could too. He was kryptonite to her. She had been brought down, and I felt like cheering. I'd never seen anyone do that before. It was like he'd killed my worst enemy, and he deserved my love and devotion. Right then, I was determined he'd have both. I followed him on to the bus, leaving her behind me.

I was in the aisle headed for Spencer, who had taken a seat in the back, when Suey clomped up the steps, holding her ear with one hand and her lunch with the other. The bag rustled as she gestured at our usual front seat. "Kent," she said, sliding in. "Up here."

"No."

She fixed me with her most baleful look, the one that always worked. Then she used the threat that always worked. "I'll tell Mom."

Spencer didn't say a word, but he held me with those eyes. He wanted me back there as much as I wanted to be there. Just looking at him and remembering how he'd vanquished her gave me courage I didn't know I had.

"Go to hell," I said. Her eyes grew saucer-wide, and she sat down heavily.

But her hold over me was broken. I plunged into the depths of the bus, leaving Suey behind for good. She knew she'd lost. She knew it as well as I knew I'd get the whipping of my life when I got home from school. For defying my sister. For cussing. But I didn't care. When I looked at him, it felt like finding the right piece of a jigsaw puzzle. When he moved his now-dented lunchbox and scooted over to make room for me, we fitted together perfectly.

THE CIRCUS

he bejeweled edges of my grandmother's cat's-eye sunglasses sparkled in the sun as she glanced at Spencer and me in the rearview mirror. We sat in the backseat of her enormous black Eldorado. "You boys okay back there?"

We didn't have our hands down each other's pants the way we usually did. But we squirmed, bumping into one another, giggling.

"Nobody has to pee? Kent?"

"No, ma'am," I said.

"I do a little, Miss Lee." Everyone in town, including her family, called her Miss Lee.

She gave a slight chuckle. "I might have known—I swear, you are the peeingest thirteen-year-old boy I ever saw, Spencer. How many Cokes did you have before we left?"

"Only one, ma'am. But my mom says it's not the Coke that makes you pee. It's the rum."

I heard little amusement in Miss Lee's brief laugh. Spencer was not shy about his mom being an alcoholic. If anything, he reminded people often to see how they'd react. Not for pity.

7

Maybe respect because he still managed to make himself breakfast, go to school, get dinner and finish his homework on the days she couldn't get out of bed or off the sofa, but if he got a whiff of anyone's pity, he'd clam up.

"Well, unless it's an emergency, you can wait until we arrive." A horn blared behind us. "Hold your damn horses," Miss Lee shouted out the open window. Despite the recent April snowstorm, the temperature in Denver was mild—well, milder than the high country where we lived, which is why she had the window down. She turned back to the wheel and inched the car forward. "I can smell the elephants. Won't be long now, boys."

We were headed to the circus. Spencer had seen the ad in the *Post*. But we couldn't count on her to get tickets, and she always wanted Spence to stick around the house. Besides, my mom forbade me from ever being in a car "that woman" drove.

I dared to ask at dinner.

"The *circus?*" Mom said, her eyebrows arching as she dished out overcooked peas and carrots. "Honestly, Kent—do you think we're made of money?"

"I'll pay. I got money saved up from chores and stuff."

"Don't say 'stuff.' It's imprecise."

"So can we go if I pay?"

"I don't think your father wants to drive clear downtown just to go to a circus. Do you, Dan?" She shoved a platter of pork chops at him.

Dad took a deep breath and speared a couple of chops. "No dear. I don't think so." My father had two voices: the subdued murmur he used around her and his real voice—the one he used when he was alone with us or he was fixing the car and

8

talking to himself. The older we got, the less we heard that one.

Mom turned to my sister. "You don't want to go, do you Suey?"

Suey shook her long red hair back and picked up the pansy-bordered bowl of mashed potatoes. "No, ma'am."

"Well, there you are then."

"Oh, for Lord's sake, Bernice," Miss Lee said. Tonight was one of the occasions she ate dinner with us at the little house. It's not any smaller than most of the other homes in town, but across the way is her place, a real mansion built by Mister Lee. He'd made enough in mining to buy the whole mountain and build a home, but that didn't stop one of those mines from collapsing on him before he was thirty. "It's a circus, not a holiday in France. I'll take the boy." She turned to me and smiled. "Why don't you ask your friend Spencer to come along?"

Mom paused in pouring herself a glass of iced tea. "Mother, we're trying to discourage that relationship."

"Spencer's a little *queer*," Suey said.

"He is not!"

"*Kent!*" Mom slammed the pitcher of iced tea down on the table top. I noticed my father did not even jump but kept his eyes down at his plate. "Can't we have at least one dinner without unpleasantness? You know how I feel about shouting at the table." Mom unfolded her napkin and placed it in her lap, side-eyeing Miss Lee. "If you intend to take the boys to the circus, I won't stop you. But I want you to keep a close eye on them, do you understand?"

"As if I have never raised children of my own? Did I not take you to the circus enough, Bernice?"

9

Mom reddened as she picked at the peas and carrots on her plate. "I notice," she said after a few bites, "you didn't bother to invite your granddaughter on this little outing."

"Suey already said she didn't want to go, but if she's changed her mind, I'll be happy to take her along. Do you want to go?"

Hesitation filled Suey's eyes as she balanced an evening out of the house against Mom's disapproval. I knew which one she'd choose. She smiled sweetly and took a piece of bread off the stack, buttering every square centimeter before she answered. "No thank you, ma'am."

Such a toad.

"Well then, I'll call May D&F tomorrow and get three tickets for Saturday. Maybe we'll even stop at Farrell's for ice cream after."

As we wound up the circular parking structure adjacent to the arena, I hoped Miss Lee hadn't forgotten her promise of ice cream. "These things are so confusing," she muttered. "When I was here for Billy Graham last winter, I just about lost the car. Tell you what, boys—we'll go clear on up to the top and take the elevator down."

She wheeled the Eldorado three more levels up the winding incline, finally emerging onto a vast concrete plain of yellow-bordered parking spots. Only one other car was parked on the whole level, a baby blue VW bug with pink and purple flowers painted over large patches of rust. Its owner, a long-haired guy dressed in a tie-dyed t-shirt and jeans, was already waiting for the elevator.

"He must be one of those hippies I read about," Miss Lee said as she pulled into a spot close to the elevator. "He doesn't look dangerous to me." I think Miss Lee saw danger differently than Mom, maybe because of her age or how wealthy she was. Mom would have made us stay in the car until he was out of sight, but Miss Lee did no such thing. She snatched up her black handbag and got out of the car, Spencer and I scrambling after her.

"Young man," she called out as the elevator door opened, "would you hold that elevator, please?"

Her gait was swift and purposeful. She leaned forward as she walked, as if anxious to arrive. Her short arms and long legs pumped together, driving her forward like a steam engine with steel grey hair. A quick, ready smile softened her aggressive posture—a flash of friendliness outlined in ruby red lipstick. Miss Lee wore makeup like she meant it.

The hippie guy held the elevator for us as instructed, returning Miss Lee's smile. His brown mutton chops were sharply defined, but the rest of his face was stubble, and the ropy veined arm that braced the door open was matted with thick brown hair. He wore one peace symbol on a leather thong around his neck, and another formed the buckle of his macramé belt. The elevator door closed with a rickety clang.

"Are you a hippie, young man?" Miss Lee asked.

He seemed surprised by the question. "I guess so. I mean, I'm against the war and all."

Miss Lee lowered her rhinestone sunglasses and looked him up and down, from his long hair to his tire-tread sandals.

"Well, who isn't against people dying?" she said. "You look like a nice enough boy to me—dressed a little different...but then when I was your age, the clothes I wanted to wear gave my parents a stir. Are you on your way to the circus?"

"Yes, ma'am."

She held one finger up and rummaged in her purse until she came up with a ten-dollar bill, which she held out to him. "Here, then. Take this and get yourself a hot dog or something. Lord knows you look like you could use a meal or two."

He didn't reach for it. "Thanks, ma'am, but..."

I hoped she'd have some money left for ice cream. "But me no buts," she said, shaking her head as she shoved the money in his hand. "And when you spend it, remember that old folks aren't all sheep. Some of us like to make up our own minds." The elevator doors opened. "Enjoy the circus, young man. Come on, boys."

We filed out, joining a meager press of people headed for one of three tired looking ticket takers dressed in faded red suits at the entrance. Hippie Guy went to one of the other ones, waving to us as he went inside. Miss Lee was still looking for our tickets in her purse. "Now, where did I...oh, here they are."

"Portal B," the red suit intoned, looking at the tickets Miss Lee had handed him. "Straight ahead, then down to your left."

"Come along, boys," Miss Lee said as we shuffled through the turnstile. "Let's go find our seats."

The portal ring went all the way around the hall, lined with red and gold colored caramel corn pushcarts, hot dog vendors, snack bars, and booths selling posters and souvenir booklets. The salty tang of fresh-popped popcorn wafted from one direction while the hot spun sugar smell of cotton candy came from another, all floating on the buzz and hum of the barker's voices. Spencer grabbed my arm, and we followed Miss Lee down portal B.

The portal noise seemed lost in the cavernous space as we entered. Looking directly down to the arena floor, I saw three rings tan with sawdust. Props and boxes of various shapes, sizes, and colors were set off to the sides, and spotlights of blue, yellow, and orange swept the rings, nearly lost under the white glare of the house lights. Workmen ferried cables and cords from one ring to another, pausing occasionally to hoist some high in the air where they hung like unfinished spider webs.

Miss Lee kept going down closer and closer to the floor, until she finally reached the first bank of seats nearest to the center ring. The usher checked her stubs against the row number and waved us into the second row. "Well, aren't these lovely seats?" she said. "We'll be sure to see everything from here, won't we boys?"

"Yes, ma'am," Spencer said. "I've never been so close to any show in my life."

"Me either. Thank you for bringing us, Miss Lee."

"You're welcome." She fished in her purse again, bringing out two more ten-dollar bills. "Here's a little something for each of you. The show won't start for a half hour, so you two can go gallivanting around if you want. Just bring Miss Lee a plain hot dog and a Coke with lots of ice. And be back here on time, hear? If I have to come looking for you, you'll wish I'd never found you. Now, scat. I've got reading to do." She dove back into her purse and retrieved a large print edition of Reader's Digest, which she propped up on her lap.

"Gee, thanks!" I said.

"Yeah, thanks!" Spencer chimed in. "Race ya."

We flew up the steps, cutting around a peanut vendor carrying a huge tray of hot salted nuts. As usual, I beat Spencer by a mile. Even though we were the same age, I was six inches taller. I was faster, stronger, and better at softball than he was, but nobody was as fearless as Spencer Michalek. He said things out loud that I only dreamed of having enough guts to say, and he tried just about anything whether he could do it or not. I watched him mount the last few steps, his longish jet-black hair flopping, and his eyes squinched shut from exertion. I knew what they looked like by heart, though. They were the bluest of blues—intense when he was asking one of his outrageous questions in class but achingly sincere when he told me how much he liked me. And he told me a lot.

"Beat ya," I said as he gained the top step.

He shrugged and grinned, showing off the front tooth he'd chipped when his mom threw him off the porch. "So? I like runnin' anyway. Let's get a hot dog."

"Okay, I said. "I gotta pee bad, though. I think there's a bathroom over by where we came in."

We peed, washed our hands, and rejoined the commotion. The place was a riot of smells. Straight from the soap and sanitizer of the bathroom into the yeasty, salty exhaust of a hot pretzel machine, we seemed to carom from stall to stall—peanuts, saltwater taffy, caramel apples on flimsy-looking sticks, chocolate bananas, and the hot whirr of the cotton candy machine—until the greasy odor of frying meat hit us, and there it was.

The snack bar.

A dizzying array of hot dogs rotated lazily on roller racks under hot lamps, a short order cook flipping burgers on the grill and dropping baskets of fries and onion rings into the hot oil that seemed to permeate everything. We both took a couple of wrapped hot dogs off the racks and gave our money to a tired-looking lady at the cash register, who returned our change as listlessly as she'd taken the bills. I almost felt bad making her move. We took our food to the condiment station and started loading up.

Spencer and I did disagree on a few things that mattered. Like hot dogs. I had already covered half the wiener with pale green chunks of relish when he asked, "How much are you gonna put on that thing?"

"Hey, you don't get much on these little spoons," I said. "You want some?" I knew the answer already.

He wrinkled up his nose. "Makes me gag." He liked his hot dogs almost plain, decorated by six tiny dots of mustard—three on each side—between the dog and the bun. I scooped one last spoonful of relish on mine, then we took our Cokes and sat down at the gleaming stainless-steel counter of the snack bar.

"Hey, do the cook guy," Spence said.

"Right now?"

"Yeah."

He loved when I made stories up about people. He was the first to clap when I read a story I wrote for class.

I watched him work the grill and serve customers. He didn't have a name tag, but he looked sort of Italian—dark-skinned, with a bushy black moustache and muscled, hairy arms. He became Mario to me. After that, the rest was easy.

"He hits his wife," I said. "That's her at the cash register. She's gonna have a baby, so she looks tired. They live in a little two room apartment down on Colfax that smells like sweat and garlic. He hates his crappy job at the grill and thinks one day he might bring in a gun and shoot the next guy who asks for extra onions on his burger."

Spence nodded as he bit into the hot dog, a dollop of mustard lodging itself at the corner of his mouth. He didn't lick it away. I wanted to. Right there. I wanted to I wanted to take his face in my hand, brush the hair away from his forehead and protect him forever. We'd live together in my room, laughing and dancing to my Beatles records, as close to each other as the orange and yellow swirls on the record label, and we wouldn't come out for anyone. Not mom or dad or Suey or our stupid teachers or Spencer's drunk mom. And at night, we'd snuggle under the big blue and white checked comforter on my bed, and he'd fall asleep with his head on my chest. I'd hear him breathing, and I'd know he was happy. And I'd be happy.

"Kiss me," he said, a dare in his voice. *Had he known what I was thinking?*

"Right here?"

"Right here."

"Spence, there are about a jillion people around."

"So?"

I was sunk, and he knew it. I couldn't resist his eyes any more than I could change the color of the sun or make my sister like me. I tried to shut out everyone around us, focusing on that blob of mustard nestled in the corner of his mouth. Pulling him close, I licked at it softly then pressed my mouth to his. Our tongues danced together, moving in secret ritual. His hands crept up my back, and he melted into me. Flares shot up in sparks behind my closed eyelids. Nothing existed for me except the moment, the kiss, the feel of his body next to mine.

Rough hands gripped our arms. I opened my eyes to see Mario shouting, "Get the hell outta here. I don't want none of that shit at my counter. Go on, get out!" He shoved us off our stools, and we fell to the concrete in a clumsy tangle.

Spencer was up on his feet again in a flash, his middle finger out and proud. "Fuck you. You can kiss my *ass!*"

Thousands of people seemed to stop and stare, clucking their tongues and shaking their heads. They trapped us, hemming us in. I could feel their hate, and I expected blows to begin falling from behind me any second. Mario's face twisted with rage, his dark eyes darting around the counter in search of a weapon. He didn't find one. "Get outta my sight." Spittle flew as he screamed.

Spencer turned his back on the counter. "Let's go. But don't run. That's what they want." His glare melted a path through the crowd like Superman's heat vision, and I forced my unsteady legs to walk beside him.

"God damn," I said as we left the buzz behind us.

"Let's get Miss Lee her hot dog and Coke at that snack bar on the other side of the portal. Do we have enough money left to get her one of those souvenir programs? I think she'd like that."

The animal acts bored the crap out of me. The lions and tigers looked drugged, the elephants were old and slow, and the trained poodles in hats gave me the creeps. The horses were pretty cool, though—strong and graceful as they circled the inside of the center ring bearing two women whose smiles gleamed brighter than their sequined leotards. The women arched their backs, pointed their toes, and did their tricks, but I paid more attention to the horses. I loved watching their taut haunches and lean, muscular flanks as they trotted around the ring, keeping their dignity despite the stupid red feathered headdresses they wore.

Spencer seemed to enjoy everything, though. He laughed at the stale, baggy-pants routines of the clowns, squealing as one came toward us and showered us with a bucket of confetti that was supposed to be water. Even Miss Lee whooped at that, shaking cut squares of paper out of her hair as she giggled.

Two men in white tights and no shirts walked the high wire. One was blondish and the other brown-haired, but they were both solidly built and hairy-chested. Spencer sneaked his hand into mine. I know Miss Lee saw it. She looked twice, but she didn't say anything. She just watched the men on the high wire like everybody else.

When they were finished riding their bicycle across the wire and doing their handstands, they tumbled down into the net that stretched beneath the wire. Gripping the edge with both hands, they flipped to the sawdust below with a grand flourish and bowed. As the crowd cheered, they began shaking hands with people in the front row.

Spencer and I jumped into the aisle and made two short

hops to the front. I shook hands with the brown-haired one, surprised at the cool dryness of his grip until I saw the white resin dusting his hand. His chest was a furry Viking breastplate, solid and impenetrable. He said something to me in a language I didn't understand, but it didn't matter. I was speechless anyway.

They backed into the center of the ring again and with a final bow, the lights went off and they were gone.

"I got to shake his hand," I said as we went back to our seats.

"I just wanted a closer look."

The ringmaster directed our attention to the far-right ring where a blond woman in plain blue tights climbed a thick rope. She put her slippered feet in two loops and began a horizontal spin. Spencer nudged me and pointed up to the top of the arena where men high up on the catwalk unfastened the trapeze bars, letting them swing free. Some other workmen were disassembling the safety net the high-wire walkers had just used.

"Why are they taking the net down?" I asked.

"I read about this in the paper," Spence said. "It's a trapeze act called 'The Netless Wonders'—three guys and a girl who perform without a net. It used to be two girls, but one got dropped in Boston."

"Did it kill her?'

"It didn't say. Probably."

The blond on the rope was now spinning by a thick ponytail she had knotted up into one of the two loops, her arms and legs extended. The applause was polite and scattered. We watched the men drop the net and roll it up, and by the time they were done, she had flipped over and was spinning by a bit she held between her teeth.

"This is boring," Spencer said to me a little too loud. "Now, if they had a guy spinning by his dick, that'd be cool."

Miss Lee must have heard him, because she pursed her red lips and looked like she was going to say something I'd regret hearing. But all she said was, "Thank you again for the souvenir program, boys. It was very thoughtful."

Spence turned red and I knew he knew he'd been overheard. Miss Lee was so easy to be with that sometimes we forgot she was there. We repeated our thanks for her bringing us to the circus, I pinched hard Spencer's leg for good measure, and we watched the blond lady shinny down the rope. Her exit music was louder than the applause.

Three spotlights hit the ringmaster in the center ring as he smoothed out his red tails. "Laydeeees and gen-tle-mennnn," he announced, "risking their lives high above your heads, performing without the safety of a net, I present to you those daredevil aerialists, The Netless Won-derrrrs."

The band blared and four figures bounded from the wings, all dressed in spangled white jumpsuits with no sleeves. I could tell from their square jaws and high foreheads that two of the three men were father and son, but I wasn't sure who I thought was better looking. The son filled out his jumpsuit with more smooth chest muscle, but the older guy wasn't built bad either. He carried himself with more authority than his son, putting his hands on the girl's waist, lifting her high in the air and letting her drop down to the ground again.

They raced to the rope ladders the workmen had thrown down from the catwalk, and they climbed toward the platforms at either end of the arena. I didn't get a good look at the odd guy, but the girl was really pretty. She didn't look related to the father and son. I had a hard time figuring things like that out with women, though.

Maybe she and the odd guy are married, I thought. She's bringing him into the act, carrying on the family tradition. And the lady who got dropped in Boston was her sister. Or maybe the lady who got dropped was his wife, and he was staying on with the act because he didn't know what else to do. There were a bunch of possibilities, but I didn't think too hard about them because Spencer hadn't asked me to make anything up about them. Once you get used to making stuff up, though, it's kind of hard to stop.

Three trapezes hung down from the rigging, two on either end for the catchers and one in the middle for whoever was flying, usually the girl. Sometimes the odd guy flew and sometimes he caught, but mostly the old man and his son did the catching. Their arms were long and sturdy, with yellow bands around their wrists. I figured the yellow was something the flyers aimed at when they were being caught.

As I watched them do full turns and half turns and somersaults, I thought how great it must be to fly through the air without a plane, knowing someone waited on the other side to catch you. Which would be better? Flying or being caught? The only two people in the whole world I'd trust to catch me were sitting right beside me. And I'd catch them when they needed it, too.

The action overhead slowed down as the band fell silent. Everyone went to the platforms except the old man. He hoisted himself upright and sat on the trapeze, wiping his hands on his resin bag. "Laydeees and gen-tle-mennnnn," said the ringmaster, "The Netless Won-derrrrrs will now attempt the infamous quad-ruuuple somersault. We must ask you for ab-so-lute silence for this feat. Please do not break their con-cen-tra-tion."

The girl waited on the far-right platform, her hands on the trapeze, while the old man pumped his legs to get some momentum before sinking down to his catching position. He called out a number or a word or something, and she launched herself off the platform. They both swung back and forth a few times, then he clapped. On her next upward swing, she let go of the bar and rocketed up to the very top of the arena.

She tucked in her arms and legs as she came back down, the old man at his farthest point from her. As he swung back toward her, she began to somersault. She completed four full revolutions, then gracefully—not in any hurry, it seemed—extended her arms to be caught. He came up quickly beneath her. In the hush of the arena, we heard their flesh slap when they made contact.

I remember letting out my breath with relief, but as her full weight came down on their grip, their right hands separated. Amidst gasps from the audience, she panicked and began to flail. Suddenly, she was in free fall, a blurred streak of white tumbling toward the same spot where I'd shaken the wire walker's hand. We heard her spine crack as she landed face up on the wall of the ring. She bounced into some empty seats in the front row, her limp arms and legs draped awkwardly over the armrests before she fell to the floor.

Before I knew it, Spence was out of his seat picking his way down the same path he'd seen to the wire walkers. "Help!" he screamed as he bounded across seats and skittered down the rows. "Help!" I followed because I wanted to see too. I could sense Miss Lee behind us, but she had no hope of catching up.

We were the first ones there. Her blue eyes were open, but they didn't look like anybody's eyes anymore. They looked like the fake eyes on my old teddy bear. Spence was crying and trying to hold her head up, her hair falling through his fingers. I thought I saw something leave her and hover overhead a moment before vanishing, but I couldn't focus long enough to tell for sure. Was that her spirit? A ghost? Or was it just a trick of the lights?

A bunch of adults all got there at the same time and crowded around us, pushing us out of the way. Miss Lee took our hands and pulled us away from the scene, standing in the aisle as the grownups massed around the dead girl. The band started playing, and another act came out on the other side of the ring, far away from what was going on.

"I think I'd better get you boys home," Miss Lee said in the softest voice I'd ever heard her use.

No one said much on the way back home. Spencer stared out of the right window in the back seat, and I stared out the left. Our hands met in the middle occasionally, and we'd interlace our fingers or rub them together. I didn't remember the ice cream until we were far away from Denver, but I didn't really want to stop anyway.

I couldn't quit thinking about how the trapeze lady was

there one minute, smiling and bowing and waving, and then she was gone. And the scary part was she'd never come back. Ever. I remember thinking it would happen to Spence. And Miss Lee. And I didn't know how I'd ever go on without them, probably like that lady's kids or mom or dad or whatever didn't know how they'd go on without her. But I guessed you just did, like Miss Lee did after the mine collapsed on Mister Lee.

It wasn't like the deaths in Sherlock Holmes or Agatha Christie or Nero Wolfe or even the ones on TV. Somebody was either already dead when the story started or you could figure out pretty quick who was gonna croak and why. And on TV, the dead people all came back to life on other shows. This was different. She hadn't blackmailed or killed anybody or done anything bad that I knew about. All she did was fly. And you shouldn't die because of that. It wasn't right. Or was it? Maybe that's just how things were.

Once we got to the mountain, we pulled off U.S. 40 on to the service road and started up to the caretaker's cabin where Spence and Shirley lived. Miss Lee slowed the car down. "I don't see any lights," she said. "Are you sure your mother's home?"

Spence shifted around in the backseat. He looked like he had to pee again. "She's probably asleep, ma'am."

"Passed out on the sofa, more like," Miss Lee muttered under her breath. "Well, if she's asleep, we probably shouldn't disturb her. I think you should come with me and spend the night at the big house," she said, pressing the accelerator and driving by. "You too, Kent."

"Mom won't—"

"I'll talk to your mother, don't worry. You can both spend

the night in Kent's room. Won't that be fun?"

"Yes, ma'am," Spence said, grinning briefly before he went back to his thinking face. We wouldn't be doing anything under the covers tonight. We never did when he was thinking about something. He'd stare and look distracted and not say much of anything at all. When he was finished thinking, though, he was tough to shut up.

Miss Lee drove us up the mountain, ushering us quickly in the front door of the big house. We all took off our coats and boots in the entry hall. Miss Lee hung her scarf up and put her purse down. "Are you boys hungry?"

"No, ma'am," Spence said. He was never hungry when he was thinking.

"There's apple pie and milk in the kitchen," she encouraged. I wanted some, but I didn't want to leave Spence alone. "Maybe we'll just go to bed," I said.

She sighed. "Well, you two have had a long day. Are you sure there's nothing you want to talk about?"

Spence and I both shook our heads.

She smiled at us. "Off to bed with you now," she said, sweeping us upstairs as she went to the phone nook by the banister. "We'll have a big breakfast and a long talk in the morning. Goodnight, boys."

We went to my room without saying anything. I knew better than to try and talk to him when he was like this, though I hadn't seen him this bad since the time his mom went to Denver and disappeared for two weeks. We both undressed in silence and climbed in bed. Spence was asleep in minutes, but I couldn't close my eyes. I got up and padded around the room in my underwear, looking out the window at the moon shining high over the tops of the trees. I went to the desk and ran my hands over the books I kept at Miss Lee's—the ones I used to have at home before Mom thought I outgrew them—Nancy Drew, the Hardy Boys, Tom Swift. But the answer I was looking for wasn't in those. If it had been, I wouldn't still be looking. I'd already know.

Maybe death was one of those things I couldn't understand until I wrote about it. Sometimes that happened. I sat down at my desk and took a notebook out of the middle drawer. I quietly tore out the pages that had something on them because I wanted a clean notebook for this. What would I call it? I couldn't start without a title. I got up again, the skin of my bare back sticking to the chair, and paced some more and looked out the window some more, but I couldn't write anything. I didn't even know her name, and I didn't want to make up stuff about her. This would have to be the truth. I'd wait until tomorrow's newspaper came out. I closed the notebook, printed the most obvious title I could think of on the cover—*The Dead Book*—and put it on the nightstand next to the bed. Folding my arms around Spencer, I drew him close to me and closed my eyes.

THE 12:40 TO CHICAGO

July 6, 1971

Like any fourteen and fifteen-year-old boy, Spence and I were driven by dicks—endlessly fascinated by them, both ours and anyone else's we could see. Our wanking bordered on fanaticism, both separately and with each other. But we could never do it at my house because we were too closely monitored, and it was a dicey proposition even staying over at the big house. Miss Lee kept us occupied during the day, and she always put us in the room next to her at night. When we did fool around, we always had to be conscious of the noise. We weren't sure how she'd react if she caught us, but we didn't want to lose the only friend we had.

Sometimes we did it at Spence's house in his tiny room, but only when we were sure Shirley had passed out on the living room sofa. Even then, she would sometimes rouse herself to rummage through the little airline bottles she kept in the medicine cabinet. Exceptions to the rule happened, but we largely confined our sexual escapades to a small cave on the town side of the mountain.

It was about fifteen or twenty feet deep and tall enough for an adult to stand up in. We had brought in a propane stove for beans and weenies and a smallish pallet to put it on since the floor was often damp. We had blankets and flashlights and naturist magazines we'd cadged from one of the high school guys. Lots of flopping penises in black and white. We used to call our sojourns there "going camping." The entrance was easily hidden by a big bush of brambles we'd dragged over from the other side of the trail. If Suey hadn't followed us that day, we'd have never gotten caught.

We faced the expected recriminations, but threats and warnings were nothing new. However, Mom's white-hot anger and desperation was worse than ever. Her voice had a finished-with-it-all strain that said more than her words. And Miss Lee was strangely reticent to intercede in our behalf as she'd done in the past. She just let Mom go on, egged on by Suey, who was absolutely traumatized by the tawdriness of what she'd witnessed—for almost twenty minutes.

"Maybe you boys ought to hold back for a while," Miss Lee suggested. "Not see each other for a few weeks until things calm down."

But to two lovestruck teenagers, a few weeks is tantamount to decades apart, and our adolescent defiance came to the fore. It was time for the Chicago plan.

We had devised the Chicago plan a few years back. We'd hop a bus to Denver, buy a ticket to Chicago, and never look back. Why Chicago? Spence said because Chicago was bigger than Denver but not as big as New York City. Though I was a year older—for eight months of the year anyway—he was always the man with the plan. My job was to figure out a way to carry them through, but the Chicago adventure was a team effort.

One of the many problems was funding, but where there's a plan, there's a budget. Miss Lee's kitchen drawer—third left of the silverware—was always stuffed with tens, twenties, and fifties she kept around the house to pay odd jobs or delivery boys or put in her purse when she was late getting out of the house. Every once in a while, she'd have us count it and try to straighten it out, but the next time we saw it, it'd be a tangled mess usually worth about five to seven hundred dollars. More than enough to get us to Chicago.

"It's time," I told him over the phone. I'd been forbidden to call him, but no one was home.

"Now?" He was always ready to go. No hesitation.

"This weekend," I said. "Mom and Suey are leaving Saturday for Grand Junction to visit Aunt Carla for her birthday. I can't go because I'm grounded—like I'd want to anyway. They're out getting a present right now. I just have to figure out a way to empty the drawer without Miss Lee finding out for a while. When she sees her stash is gone, she'll know something's up and come looking for us before they get back."

"So, when do we go?"

"I'll check out what times the Denver bus comes both Saturday and Sunday, but be packed and ready to go. Once I get the cash, we're not gonna have a lot of time."

"Cool. I'll be ready," he said.

"I'll get a night bus. You know how early Miss Lee goes to bed."

"Right on. You're pretty good at this."

"I learned everything I know from you."

He chuckled. I loved to make him laugh. Still do. "Hey, wait," he said suddenly. "We can't take the bus."

"Why not?"

"That's the first place they'll check. The key to this whole thing is getting as good a head start as possible, right? We don't have another way out of town, so they'll check the bus sure as shit. And it's not like the driver won't remember two kids getting on in the middle of the night. Shit."

"How are we gonna get down to Denver, then?"

He was silent a moment, then I almost heard the thought come into his head. "Shirley's car."

"Shirley's car? I don't even have my learner's permit yet."

"So? I can drive it. I've driven it lots of times."

"When?"

"I can drive it, don't worry. She never uses it, not with the liquor store two blocks away and her office three blocks away. It's always in the garage. By the time they think to check on it and report it, we'll be in Chicago. Twenty-two hours, man. Twenty-two hours is all we need from Denver to freedom. Once we get to Chi-town, they'll never find us. Never."

"We gotta go over mountains, Spence. Fuckin' mountains. What if we get stopped?"

"We won't get stopped."

"Do you even know the way to Denver?"

"Um, it's on a big sign on the way out of town," he said with impatience. "Look, it's perfect. Shirley starts drinking anywhere from ten to noon on a Saturday, so she'll be passed out by eight. Miss Lee will be in bed by nine. You get the money, we'll meet at the cave, hike down the back way, we get in the car and go.

Denver in two hours, Chicago in another twenty-two. Miss Lee won't notice you're gone until sometime on Sunday and probably won't do anything until your mom gets back Sunday night. We'll be home free by then."

"What'll we do with Shirley's car when we get to Denver?"

"Leave it at the station. By the time the cops will find it, it won't make any difference. We'll have a new life away from this hick town. Together. Are you with me?"

Oh, I was with him all right. I'd long ago made up my mind that I'd follow him to the ends of the earth. Chicago was nothing. I didn't care about leaving my folks, but I hated leaving Miss Lee without even saying goodbye. And I really hated stealing from her. I could only hope when we were all adults and met again, she'd understand how it had to be. She'd forgive me—us—and we'd have a good laugh about it. After we'd paid her back, of course.

Things went pretty much as we'd planned. Mom, Dad, and Suey left for Aunt Carla's house Saturday morning, and I moped around most of the day. I tried to watch cartoons and then went over to the big house and helped Miss Lee shell peas for a while. I ate dinner over there, but I was too keyed up to eat much or to be good company.

"You haven't touched your roast beef," Miss Lee remarked, looking at me over her glasses. "It's your favorite. What's wrong?"

"Nothing," I said, herding peas around on my plate.

She looked at me over her glasses, which is how I knew she meant business. "Nonsense. You're upset because you can't see Spencer, aren't you?"

"Yes'm." It was as good an excuse as any.

"I didn't say much at the time," she told me, putting her fork down, "but I knew they were going to take this trip to Carla's and we'd be alone this weekend. I figure there's nothing we can do if we're in town tomorrow morning and we just happen to run into him at Meecham's or something. I'd sit there for a while so you two could visit—but only at the restaurant. You can't be alone with each other for at least two weeks while your folks simmer down, okay?"

"Okay." I was taken aback. I had no idea what to say. She was letting us meet even though we were grounded.

She winked at me. "Why don't you call Spencer and tell him? Maybe you'll have some appetite for that apple pie for dessert."

I hoped I looked excited rather than the other ten or fifteen other emotions I'd experienced in the last thirty seconds or so. And she'd insist I use the phone right there in the dining room. I was sunk. I had no choice but to call him. He answered on the first ring.

"Already? Shirley's not out yet."

"Hey Spence," I said heartily. "Miss Lee and I are going to meet you downtown tomorrow at Meecham's. Isn't that cool?"

"What are you talki—oh. Oh. She's right there, and she was going to let us get together while your folks are out of town. Shit. I'll bet she looks proud of herself, too."

I looked over at Miss Lee, beaming as she cut a huge piece of pie for me. "You should see her face."

"No thanks." He hesitated a beat before he said what was in my head too. "We're still goin', right? You're gonna get the money after she falls asleep, and then we're leaving. If we're ever

32

gonna start our own lives, it's gotta be now."

"Yes. I…I…goodbye." I hung up the phone. I couldn't talk to him anymore. Couldn't listen to him. Couldn't say goodbye to Miss Lee, couldn't smile at her when I knew in less than an hour, I'd be stealing from her. All I could do was run from the room back across the yard to my own room in the little house, hearing her call my name. I slammed the door and sat on my bed, legs crossed, breathing hard at first, then slowing as I watched the lights in the big house. Room by room, they began to click off after a while. When the whole place was dark, I went over to the window and breathed in a huge gulp of mountain air.

I threw some clothes into my suitcase and headed outside, going around back of the big house to use the kitchen door. Miss Lee never locked it. I left the bag on the back porch, opened the door and the screen door carefully and tiptoed inside. I was concentrating so hard on crossing the kitchen floor quietly that I nearly didn't see the note she'd left under a plate with the pie on the table. I had to stop and read it:

Dear Kent:

I don't know what I said, but I'm sorry. I truly am. You boys have enough to deal with. I wish I could make your folks under-stand, but people only see what they want to see. One day, they'll see you like I do. Until then, all I can do is love you both.

Miss Lee

Tears came to my eyes, and I wiped my eyes and nose with my t-shirt, trying not to sniffle in case she was sleeping in her chair in the library. I put the pie back down on the note with the point of the piece facing the way it was when I picked it up. I didn't want her to know I'd been back. She'd think I was still mad or hurt or whatever and wouldn't be looking for me right away tomorrow. It'd be a while before she figured out we were gone.

I eased the drawer open soundlessly and began stuffing my pockets with bills, trying to be fold them up quietly at first but then just cramming them in until my jeans and my jacket bulged. I wanted to finish up and get out of there. I told myself it was so she didn't catch me, but the truth was, I felt guiltier the longer I stayed. Maybe once I was gone from the big house and off the mountain, it'd get better.

Finally, I emptied the drawer right down to the green contact paper she'd lined it with. Every pocket I had was jammed with money. I gave each of them one final scrunchdown to make sure I didn't lose any. Not only were we going to need every dollar I could steal, I didn't want to leave a trail down the mountain. I zipped my outside and inside jacket pockets shut, closed the drawer, and eased my way across the floor and out the door.

Outside, where I could move more freely, I scrunched the money down again, then I took one last look at Miss Lee's house and headed the back way down the mountain. The moon was three-quarters full, and a gentle breeze soughed through the pines and aspens. I knew the way even without the faint path worn through the woods, but I didn't hurry. I wanted to be quiet and take my time. Who knew when I'd see the mountain again?

I shivered despite my jacket, a cold wave of homesickness washing over me when I hadn't even left yet. This was the start of a new life. Me and Spence on our own at last in the big city, something we'd dreamed about and planned for and talked about in vague terms ever since we'd been together. Away from this town, out with people who were like us. We knew they were out there. And we were finally going to do it. If Shirley passed out on schedule. If Spence got the car. If he could start it and it had gas. If nobody caught us or found out until it was too late. If we didn't get stopped on the way to Denver or even while we were there. So many things could happen, but it would all be okay. We were together.

"How much?" Spence asked.

I stopped adding in my head to answer him. "I'm not finished yet." I had twenties and tens stuck under my right leg and fifties under my left and was sorting them as I went, putting the fives and ones in the open glovebox that illuminated my task. I figured we'd split the fives and ones for spending money on the trip and save the rest for fares and seed money for when we got to Chicago.

Spence fiddled with the radio a while, but you can never get anything but static for more than a few miles in the high country. He snapped it off and looked over at me. At least I thought he was looking at me. "The moon sure looks cool goin' in and out of the trees," he said. "You gonna miss the mountains?"

"I guess." Twenty-forty-sixty-eighty-one hundred, twenty-forty-sixty, eighty, one hun—

"Are you okay? You haven't said much since we left."

"I'm counting." Twenty-for—

"Yeah, now you are. You weren't for the first half-hour, and you didn't say much then either."

I put that two hundred in the stack of twenties under my right leg and tried to glare at him, but I couldn't. He looked too concerned about my mood for me to be mad at him. "I'm cool," I told him. "I just feel crappy about taking money from Miss Lee, that's all." I didn't tell him about the note.

"We're gonna pay it back when we can," he insisted. "We're not stealing it. How much did we get?"

"I still have a couple of pockets to count, but it's a lot."

"Enough to take the train instead of the bus?"

"Probably, yeah. Why?" I started getting a prickly feeling up my spine. "I thought we were gonna take the bus. Trains have conductors and you gotta get your ticket punched and all that. With the bus, you just get on and nobody cares."

"The train would be fun. A bus is just a bus, man."

His mind was made up. I could tell. My only chance was a delaying tactic until I could come up with a good argument. "Hang on and let me finish counting this." I emptied my last two pockets, smoothed out the bills, and sorted them. No tens or twenties this time—they were all fifties. I breathed out. "We got over twelve hundred bucks," I said.

"You sure?"

I nodded. "Twelve hundred and forty-seven dollars. Miss Lee doesn't usually keep that much in the house. She must have gone to the bank, forgot she had money in the drawer, and got more the next time she went to the bank."

"Cool. We can definitely afford the train."

"Why are you so fired up about the train? Is it faster?"

"It's funner."

He was avoiding the question. "But is it faster?"

"No," he admitted.

"Is it about the same?"

He sighed. "The bus is twelve hours from here to Chicago. Train's sixteen."

"Spence, that's a whole four hours longer. I thought we were trying to get there quick."

"We are, man, but...well, I've never been on a train before. Who knows when we'll get the chance again?"

"We have the rest of our lives to take the train. We should stick with the original plan and take the bus. Nobody will notice us, it's cheaper, and we'll get there sooner." I tried to sound as final as I could.

He smacked the steering wheel with his fist. "Shit," he said. I let it go. I fiddled with the money, taking the stacks from under my thighs, folding them up as well as I could, and putting them back in my pockets. I gathered the fives and ones out of the glovebox, folded them up as well, and closed it.

We sat in the darkness for a while. He turned the radio on again and tried to get some music, but every station he found was overridden by static in seconds. He turned it off again and looked over at me. "I'm sorry," he said. "You're right. It was a stupid idea."

I shrugged. "It wasn't stupid. Sounds like fun. We'll do it one of these days. Okay?" I reached out and put my hand on top of his hand, resting on the gearshift.

"Okay," he said, grinning. The moonlight shone on his

chipped front tooth, and the breath caught in my throat. His lopsided grin, the tooth, the way his long dark hair fell across his forehead. I'd do anything for him, go anywhere, face anyone. My chest swelled until I thought I was going to cry. I tried to keep it out of my voice.

"Hey," I said. "Make me a promise, willya?"

"What?"

"When I'm a famous writer, and you're a successful architect, no matter how rich we get, don't ever fix that tooth, okay?"

❧

"Two tickets for the…" I looked down at the schedule again. "…12:40 a.m. to Chicago, please."

I didn't have to explain. The balding guy in the ticket window didn't even look up from his copy of *Portnoy's Complaint*. "Forty-two fifty," he said, punching a couple of buttons on a console to the side and putting two tickets in the space under the window. He took the money, stuffed it into the cash drawer, gave me my change, and wiped his hands on the front of his white shirt. "Gate B. Leaves in a half hour." He turned the page.

Spence nudged me. "Ask him where we can get somethin' to eat."

I shook my head at Spence, took the tickets, and stepped away from the window. I unzipped my jacket pocket and put the change with the rest of our money.

"Why didn't ya ask him?" Spence said, following me.

"He was so busy reading he didn't even notice us. He'd never be able to say that two kids bought tickets to Chicago if the cops ask him, but if I made him look up from his book, he'd remember that sure as shit."

Spence tapped his temple and grinned. "Thinkin' all the time, huh?"

I loved it when he thought I was smart. "Some of the time, anyway. Hey look, I don't know if there's gonna be a bathroom on the bus or not, so we better go. You watch the bags for a minute while I go, and then it'll be your turn, okay?"

"Yeah, sure. When are we gonna get something to eat?"

"We'll figure it out when I get back." I looked around and headed for the restroom sign that pointed around the corner, hoping they weren't as broken down as the rest of the place. The orange plastic bench-chairs were gouged and broken, some of the black and white floor tiles were missing, and the whole station smelled like stale sweat and exhaust. On the way, I saw a couple of vending machines with candy and chips and stuff. That'd have to hold us. I hoped we had enough change. I didn't want to ask for any.

The signs pointed down a short hall that ended in a drinking fountain with a restroom door on either side—men's on the left, women's on the right. But there was a kid standing there looking at the framed posters on the wall. Well, he was trying to *look* like it anyway. He was a little older than us, already sprouting a passable moustache. He was in a thin white t-shirt, jeans with frayed cuffs, and scuffed, beat-up Keds. I didn't see him too well because he kept angling away from me. Keeping my distance, I went in the bathroom.

It was in even worse shape than the rest of the bus station, but at least I was the only one in there. Three floor urinals stood on one wall, streaked brown from the top to the bottom with hard water stains. At least that's what I figured they were. I didn't really want to think about the alternatives. Ever pee shy and paranoid—*what if that kid outside comes in*—I bypassed them and headed for the stalls.

But none of them had locks, just holes where they ought to have been. *At least there's walls.* Opposite them, the sink was dirty, a line of grime around its lip, and the mirror above it cracked and permanently fogged.

I took the stall closest to the wall but couldn't figure out how to keep the door shut. I couldn't leave it open, and it was too far away for me to keep closed with my hands and pee at the same time. In a flash of inspiration, I took off my jacket, hung it by the collar on the outside edge of the door so it was half in and half out of the stall, and swung the door into place. The fabric and lining brought the gap between the stall and divider into a tight fit. Well, it was still kinda loose, but it would stay closed long enough for me to pee.

Suddenly, I felt an unstoppable torrent rushing out of my bladder. I hadn't realized I needed to pee that badly. I almost didn't get it out in time, but I managed. I was peeing so hard it hurt, and I could hear the splash bouncing off the echoey tiles.

Just then the bathroom door opened. I couldn't stop the flow, but I tensed up all over and went breathless with anticipation, wanting desperately to bend over and see if his feet went over to the urinals or were marching toward the stalls. Hearing him coming toward me, I started to sweat a little bit. The shoes squeaked even closer, pausing outside the stall next to me. It was the guy from outside, I knew it. I could hear him rustling as

I continued to pee. It almost felt empty enough so I could stop it, but not quite. My scalp felt prickly from nervousness.

The tension within me grew unbearable, and when I thought I couldn't take it anymore, I heard a rustle from outside my stall. Suddenly, whoever was there jerked my jacket off the stall door. It popped outward, and I caught a glimpse of him running in the scuzzy mirror. The bathroom door banged open and shut as I realized the fucker had stolen my jacket.

Pissing all over myself, I turned around and ran right into the edge of the stall door as it swung in again, too surprised to even yell. A little stunned, my foot slipped and I went down on one knee for a second before I got to my feet again and managed to tuck myself in. I zipped up, raced to the door, tore out of the bathroom, and stood there whipping my head around without seeing anyone.

Shit, I thought. Our money. My heart and stomach sank, and I got a little dizzy. I stepped around the corner and saw Spence was sitting on one of the benches reading a brochure or something. No one with worn Keds and faded jeans was in sight. I wanted to scream, but my fear of calling attention to myself was stronger, and I choked that impulse back.

Instead, I walked up to Spence as calmly as I could. "Did you see a guy running out of the bathroom?"

He looked up. "Some guy ran out the door a few seconds ago, but I dunno where he came from. Why? And why is your front all wet? Did you pee on yourself?"

I took a deep breath to calm myself. It didn't help. "He stole my jacket."

Spence's look of confusion resolved itself into a frown. "You put the money in your pants pocket, right?"

I shook my head.

"You mean it's gone?"

"Yeah."

"Shit!" He wheeled around, looking at everyone in the room. The guy at the ticket counter still hadn't put *Portnoy* down. "Fuck. What are we gonna do now?"

He started to run for the door, but I grabbed his arm. "Wait," I hissed. "We just can't run all over the place. Everyone will notice us. Guy's probably gone by now anyway."

"Goddammit," Spence breathed. "Why..."

"Why wasn't I watching?"

"Yeah."

I explained how it happened. He didn't look as pissed as he had when I started, but he didn't look too happy, either. He kept clenching and unclenching his fists and looking around like the guy was gonna come out from around a corner any minute.

The loudspeaker blared. "Number twenty to Chicago now boarding."

"What are we gonna do, Spence?"

He closed his eyes a second, then opened them and looked at me. "We're gonna get on the bus. We got tickets, and it's not like we can go back home. We can figure out what to do when we get there. How much money we got?"

"Just a few dollars plus what change we got back from the tickets."

"I saw a coupla machines over there. Let's get somethin' for the trip with what we got. We can eat a little and think when we get goin.'"

"I'm sorry, Spence."

He shook his head. "It's not your fault. Don't worry. Lemme think about it." He reached out to hug me, but I shied away.

"I don't think that'd be too smart right now. C'mon, let's go."

We picked up our bags and went outside through the boarding exit. The stench of gasoline and fumes was thick, and I could smell the grime on the concrete. I looked up for a second, but I couldn't see the stars like I could on the mountain. I searched the legs all around me for those Keds and frayed jeans, but I didn't see him. The driver was standing by the bus steps taking tickets and putting suitcases into a big compartment on the side of the bus. We gave him ours and joined the few passengers embarking.

The bus was maybe about a third full. Some people were sleeping, their heads propped against the windows, but everyone who had their eyes open seemed tense and weary at the same time. A thought came to me. "We didn't get anything to eat," I said to Spence.

"Can't worry about it now. Let's go to the back." He headed for an empty seat pretty close to the back. We both slid in, him at the window and me on the aisle. The cloth seat was padded better than I'd expected—better than the school bus, anyway. This might not be so bad after all. Except we were broke. And it was my fault. If I'd just been looking out, I'd still have my jacket and things would be okay.

"Hey," Spence said quietly. He was looking at me and smiling. "We'll be fine. We still got each other, right?" He reached over and took my hand in his, squeezing it as I leaned over and started crying on his t-shirt. I wasn't loud. I was trying not to

43

attract attention, but I couldn't hold it in any longer. He patted my shoulders as they shook. "I know," he kept saying. "It'll be okay."

"What's wrong with your friend, sonny?" someone asked from the aisle beside us.

Shit. Somebody noticed us. Fear dried up my tears, and I disengaged from Spence, sniffing as I let go of his hand and ran a sleeve under my nose.

"He's not my friend, he's my brother," Spence answered, sticking with our cover story. "He's okay. Just a little homesick, that's all."

"Your brother, huh?" the man said. He was middle-aged, but from our teenage perspective, that was anyone older than thirty. His forehead was high, due to a receding brown hairline with a widow's peak. Horn-rimmed glasses sat on a bulbous nose in the middle of his round face, and beneath it was a knowing smirk I took an instant dislike to. "He don't look like you."

"We had different dads," Spence said, frowning. "What's it to you?"

The guy held up his hands, one of them holding a briefcase. "No offense, kid." He put the briefcase down in the seat in front of us and took off his tan overcoat. "Anyone sitting here?"

Spence shrugged and looked out the window as the guy sat down. But he didn't sit down with his back to us. He stretched out sideways on the seat, leaning against the window and glancing over at us every once in a while. The engine roared, and the bus pulled out of the station.

"Where you boys going to?" the stranger asked.

"This is the train to Chicago, right?" Spence said, not looking away from the window.

"Ah, ha, right," the man said with a snort. But he didn't turn away from us. "That's where I'm going. Got business there. Name's Roger," he said, putting a hand over the seat. "Roger Corwin."

I nudged Spence. "We're trying to blend in," I whispered to him.

Spence sighed and stopped staring out the window. "Name's…uh…Donnie," he said, shaking Roger's hand. "This is my brother, Ralph."

"Hi," I said.

Roger smiled. It wasn't much more wholesome than his smirk. "So, you boys got family in Chicago?"

"We're going to visit my dad," Spence said. He always wanted me to make up stuff about people, but he was pretty good at it himself. And it looked like he was on a roll. "He lives in Oak Park."

Roger looked impressed. "Oak Park? Hey, that's some money there—you rich, Donnie?"

"Not hardly. Just having a visit, that's all. Don't get to see him much."

I tried to pay attention in case Spence needed me to corroborate something or I got asked a question later, but the gentle rocking of the bus combined with the heat and the drone of the conversation put me to sleep. When I woke up, I had my head on Spence's shoulder, and they were still talking. The bus, however, had stopped.

"I was just about to wake you up," Spence said. "We're in Ogallala, Nebraska for a rest stop. Roger said he'd buy us a burger at the all-night place across the street from the station."

Roger nodded, his glasses sliding down until they hit a bump on his nose. "Yeah, they know me there. I take this bus all the time. C'mon, let's go. I'm sure you boys are as hungry as I am." He slid out of the seat, leaving his briefcase on top of his overcoat.

"Crap," I said to Spence as we got out. "What's our names again?"

"I'm Donnie, and you're Ralph."

I winced. "Ralph? Jeez, why not say I'm Melvin and scar me for life?"

"Don't complain. He's a pretty nice guy, and he's gonna buy us something to eat. Sells pool tables. Married with a couple of daughters our age, just so you know. Come on, let's eat."

And eat we did. The diner was small and didn't take long to fill with people from the bus. There was only one waitress, so the crowd kept her hopping. We sat at the counter on red vinyl stools. Roger had a cup of coffee and a BLT, and we both had burgers and fries we practically inhaled. Roger ate slowly, talking, drinking his coffee, and occasionally taking bites from his sandwich. He lit a cigarette and said he was finished with half a sandwich and all the fries left. We split them.

I could see the reflection of the neon lights in his glasses as he watched us. "Yep," he said. "Business is pretty good. Company wants me to fly this route, but I like the bus. You meet interesting fellows like yourselves, and it's cheaper. I pocket the difference, but nobody cares. As long as I get where I'm supposed to be, no one asks any questions. You boys about done? We gotta be getting back to the bus," he said as he got off the stool. and dug through his wallet for a twenty that he left on the counter. He waved at the harried waitress. "Keep the change, Annie."

She nodded and smiled at him. "Thanks, Bill."

Spence looked up at him, his brow furrowed. I was probably giving him the same look. He grinned at us and ushered us out of the booth. He went to the vending machines by the door and bought a pack of Pepto-Bismol tablets, popping four as he walked back to us. "Just a little heartburn," he said, motioning for us to go outside.

Once we closed the door, he lit yet another cigarette and buttoned his suit coat. "I can give a fake name, too," he said. "Cut the bullshit, boys. You're runaways. Nobody eats like that except kids who haven't had a meal in a while. So, what's the story?" He ran his hand down the back of Spence's long, brown hair like he was petting him, then tugged on it hard enough to make Spence wince.

I felt like I was going to throw up the food I just ate, so I didn't dare open my mouth to answer. Spence wouldn't say anything. He wouldn't even repeat the story we'd already told Roger or Bill or whatever his name was. I knew that icy stare all too well. And even though I had no experience with the look in the salesman's eye, I could tell a bad situation when I saw it. My stomach flipped over again when he spoke.

"Makes no difference," he said with a chuckle. He took a long drag off the cigarette and flicked it away, smiling as he cupped Spence's ass with one hand then let it go. He leaned in and whispered in Spence's ear loud enough so I could hear it. "Boys gotta have secrets, right? Everybody's got secrets. But I'm a fair man. I just blew twenty bucks on you two, so I figure I'm owed. Get me?"

Spence didn't say anything until the man pulled his hair again. Spence's eyes flashed as he looked over at him and nodded. I understood, too.

"Good boy," he said. "Now, let's get back on the bus. Quietly. And head for the back seat. Lots of people get off at Ogallala, so it should be nice and empty. Won't be a lot of passengers getting back on until Omaha, so we got plenty of time. Let's go." He eased Spence forward with his hand in the small of his back until we were visible from the window of the diner, then he put his hands in his pockets.

I was going to get on the bus first, but Roger grabbed my sleeve. "We go first," he said. "You sit in the seat directly in front of us." I hung back while they got on, and I followed them to the back of the bus.

Spence slid in beside Roger in the very back seat while I stood in the aisle looking at them. I didn't like it, but I didn't have much say. It was going to happen regardless. "I thought you had heartburn," I said, looking for an excuse.

"I get it a lot. I'm *used* to it," he hissed. "Sit down where I told ya to. Don't just stand there, moron. You must be the slow brother," he said, chuckling at himself.

I didn't know I was crying until I felt the tears running down my cheeks.

Spence leaned over the seat and whispered in my ear. He had no idea what was in my head and how much I resented him just then. "It'll be okay," he said. "Don't worry. Just think about Chicago."

Then Roger leaned over on the other side. I wondered if

he'd heard what Spence said. "Stop crying right now, you little shit," he warned me. "Your job is to keep a lookout and not attract attention. Remember, if we get caught, they throw us all off the bus and ship you back to whatever you're running away from, so keep your mouth shut and your eyes open."

My tears almost vaporized from the heat I felt in my face. But I did what he said. A lot of people had gotten off the bus with no new passengers getting on. A few moved up, with only one older lady in a checkered head scarf sitting the farthest back except for us, and she was in the middle. I figured we'd seem suspicious being the only ones in the very rear of the bus, but when the driver got on, he didn't even check in the rearview mirror. Without saying we were leaving, he shut the doors, started the engine, and pulled out of the parking lot headed for I-70.

Spence and Roger talked softly behind me. I couldn't tell what it was about, but I thought I heard my name a couple of times. Maybe it was my imagination. At first, I sat right in front of them, trying to block them from view until I realized no one cared. Despite Roger's earlier orders, I scooted over to the window. He never noticed.

They were still just talking, though lower and not as urgent as before. Roger's voice was actually kind of calming, and my anger and frustration drained away as the darkened cornfields flew by. Or was it wheat? I couldn't tell from the moonlight and the few streetlights I saw. Well, not streetlights because there weren't any streets. What did you call them on farms?

Boredom set in, and I soon found myself unable to keep my eyes open. I leaned on the window, its surface cool and sorta clammy on the side of my head. I don't how much longer it was—the moving scenery had erased my sense of time—but an irregular thump from Roger's seat jolted me into awareness. I closed my eyes and put my hands over my ears until all I could hear were the wheels whine as the irregular thumps settled into a familiar rhythm. It seemed to go on forever before it finally stopped.

It was over with. I wanted to look back, but I was afraid of what I might see. When I finally risked a glance, Spencer was frowning out the window with his brow up against the glass. His thinking face was on, and it probably would be for a while. Until Roger was ready again.

Roger had tipped his hat over his eyes, and he was snoring lightly out of the corner of his mouth. I tried to look out the window as well, but I couldn't keep my eyes open. I felt the weight of my head bob and bang against the window and seat as I resisted sleep. Suddenly, Roger kicked my seat twice, hard enough to wake me up.

I sat up ready to glare at him, but his right arm twitched for a second and fell still, and his head slumped forward at a weird angle. Then, he slid sideways against Spence, who was still looking out the window. Not even looking, Spence shouldered him away. Roger fell back on him again, and his head lolled a bit. His hat fell off, and his eyes were wide open and staring. That's when I knew he was dead. Spence only took a second longer to notice.

He took a deep breath, preparing to round on the guy like he usually did with bullies. As he whipped around, however, he stopped dead. His face stuck mid-grimace, and he frowned. He unclenched his fist and prodded Roger's shoulder instead of socking him. He wouldn't have gotten much of a response either way.

A worried look on his face, he grabbed Roger's wrist and checked for a pulse. Shirley had passed out so many times when he was a kid, he'd learned how to do that in case he needed to call somebody. His worried look flashed into panic, then he closed his eyes and dropped Roger's hand. He breathed quietly for a few seconds.

I leaned forward. "Wh—"

He shook his head and held up his hand. "Gimme a sec," he whispered.

I wasn't gonna argue. When he did say something, it'd be in the calm voice he used in emergencies. I was never sure if it was supposed to soothe him or me. He finally opened his eyes.

"Okay," he started, then he checked Roger's pulse again. "Goddammit, he's dead for sure. We gotta move, and you're gonna go first. Pick a seat over on the other side of the bus—"

"Which seat?"

"Any seat," he said, closing his eyes again for a second and opening them again. "Look, I got about five seconds before I start screamin' and I still gotta climb over a dead guy—just find a seat on the other side of the bus. I'll be there once I work up the nerve to do this." He exhaled deep, warm breaths I could feel on my arm, trying to keep calm. "Now, go."

I had to. He was depending on me. I looked at the other side of the bus. No reading lights on anywhere, so everyone was probably asleep. The closest person to us was a lady about a third of the way up, but she was definitely sleeping. I heard her snore. My destination was six rows behind her, three up from the empty back seat directly opposite us. I scrambled, moving silently in the dark, keeping low so as not to attract the driver's attention.

I looked toward the back once I got settled down, but outside of shadows moving indistinctly, I couldn't see much. Good. That meant no one else could see anything either. Pretty soon I started thinking about what climbing over a dead body would be like. I mean, do you do it face in or face out? What would it feel like? What parts would he have to touch? It might come up in a story or something. I'd have to ask him. The more questions I thought of, the more anxious I was for him to show up. Finally, he sidled up the aisle and slid in noiselessly next to me.

"What was it like?" I asked.

"What?"

"Climbing over Roger. Did you face him or what? Did you touch him?"

He just looked at me, his mouth open. "Do I have to talk about this right now? Could you at least wait until the dead guy smell goes away?"

"I don't smell anything."

"Maybe it's my imagination," he said, putting his hand in his jeans pocket and coming out with a roll of bills he held out to me. "But this isn't. Count it."

"Where'd you get this?"

"Out of his wallet. Right front suit pocket."

"How much?"

"Won't know until you count it," he said, thrusting it at me.

I took it and leaned over to catch much light as I could from the window as I sorted and counted the stash. "Eight hundred and fifty-four dollars mostly in fifties and twenties."

"Not bad."

"Not bad? Spence, you gotta put it back."

"Nuh-uh. You want it back, *you* put it back."

"But it's stealing."

Spence rolled his eyes. "How did we get this far, Kent? Stealing. And I fuckin' earned it, goddammit. You think it was fun touching him? It wasn't. He reeked, and I can still smell him on me. Eight hundred and fifty-four dollars' worth." He settled back in his seat, arms across his chest, which rose and fell rapidly. I wasn't sure if he was gonna cry or sock me. He didn't look like he was sure either.

I didn't know what to say, so I didn't say anything. I put the money in my pocket and stared out the window as he stared ahead—I could sort of see his reflection in the glass if I looked hard enough. The heat and anger eventually left him, adding to the suddenly suffocating atmosphere of the bus. You could feel his relief as he backed away from the edge of whatever he'd almost fallen into. *We'd* almost fallen into.

I sought his free hand with mine, finding first a thumb between the seats. I pulled it gently, and he opened his palm for me. Before he could say anything, I took the wad of money and pressed it into his hand. "You're right," I said. "You earned it."

But he pushed my hand away. "You keep it. You're the banker."

"No way. I lost it the last time."

"I trust you. I love you."

"I love you too," I said. I tried to kiss him, but he stopped me.

"I wanna take a shower first," he said, not looking me in the eye. Instead, he snuggled into my side. "Let's see if we can get some sleep before we stop in Kearney." I put my head back and closed my eyes, but I knew I wouldn't sleep. I'd seen too much to shut things off that easy. I wondered how Spence could, but his breathing didn't seem as regular as it did when he was asleep. He was faking. He was thinking. I let him.

I almost nodded off myself, but the bus began to slow and it exited the freeway, headed for a parking lot adjacent to a small outbuilding. A few people waited outside the door while the snoring lady closest to us had woken up, gathered her things and scooted over, ready to leave. The bus cut its turn a little wide and drove over a curb as it entered the parking lot, jostling the passengers. The motion pitched Roger's body out of the seat headfirst into the aisle, his glasses snapping in half as his face hit the treads on the floor.

The woman screamed, and the bus braked, throwing everyone forward. His shoulder pinned against the bottom of the seat, Roger stayed put but his hat rolled just about to where we sat. The woman was still screaming, running up the aisle as she collided with the driver, a burly guy so wide he could barely fit between the seats. He sat her down and walked past, stopping right by us.

"Hey buddy," he hollered, prodding Roger with his toe. "Shit." He bent over as well as he could, checking Roger's neck. "Fuck," he said to himself as he straightened up. He looked down at us. "You boys see what happened?"

"No sir," Spence said. Too afraid to say anything, I just shook my head.

"I'll be go to hell," the driver muttered, going back up the aisle. When he reached his seat, he locked the doors and picked up the hand mike. "Everyone please stay seated. We'll try to take care of this as quickly as we can, but no one is getting on or leaving for the moment." He ignored the groans and sighs as he fished around for another microphone, pressing a button and mumbling some numbers.

"He must be calling the bus people," Spence said. "We need to get off."

"And go where? We're surrounded by cornfields."

"Grand Island?" the driver said into the handset. "That's an *hour* away. Why the hell can't you have someone come out to Kear—wait, what?" He glanced up at us. "Yeah, two of 'em…I dunno—fourteen, fifteen, I guess…" He sighed. "Right, right. Okay. Be there as quick as we can."

The driver took off his cap, rubbed his head, and came down toward us. "You boys please move right up in back of me. Everybody, there are no facilities here for handling…um…emergencies like this, so we're continuing to Grand Island. Please see the counter person there for more information."

He ignored all the shouts, sighs, and curses, his shoulders slumped as he ushered us into the seat behind his. He sat back down, strapped himself in, and took off, running over the same curb in his haste to leave. Roger's hat slid beneath the seats.

The horizon seemed limitless as we stared at it through the windshield from the front seat of the bus. After a while, the lights of Grand Island appeared in the distance, but before them a bright blur near I-80. As we neared, it became a blue and red roiling boil of lights like the nucleus of the atomic particle we saw in that Disney cartoon about nuclear energy in science class. And we were headed straight for it.

Dawn broke. It was over. Our adventure had lasted less than seven hours, with one dead pedophile in the back of a Greyhound bus and his bankroll in the left front pocket of my jeans. Our families might never forgive us. But we had to be together. They'd see that in time, or at least that was the hope I conjured. Until then, all we could do was endure. We'd been pretty good at that so far. "What are we gonna tell 'em?" I asked Spence.

He was looking at the nucleus too. "The truth. What else we got?"

THE INCIDENT

October 5th, 1971

I don't remember much about the hospital stay afterward except that lots of doctors asked me lots of questions, and I wasn't sure I was getting any of the answers right. They approached me in groups, whispering in hushed consultation before they began to ask me things:

How are you feeling today, Kent?

Is that a new shirt you have on, Kent?

How are things at home, Kent?

Their tact and carefulness suffocated me. It made me feel more apart than being queer ever did. It made me feel crazy, which is what the kids called me when I got back to school. Which is what I was. After all, I had tried to kill myself.

I couldn't see much point to living if I couldn't see Spencer anymore, and everyone clamped down after they caught us in Chicago. When Mom wasn't watching me, Suey was. And Miss Lee sat on her porch, her eyes glued to our front door. I was locked in my room at night and the window nailed shut. Phone privileges were a pipe dream. And even worse, Miss Lee hadn't spoken to either of us since they brought us back home. She didn't even talk then. She just sat in a seat by herself on the train, occasionally looking over, hurt and betrayal on her face as Mom lectured and berated us. She met any direct entreaties for help or reassurance with a stony countenance I'd never seen before. I truly wanted to die.

How to do it was the next question. I'd never shot a gun before and didn't want to miss. Hanging myself seemed too complicated, and I'd read somewhere that the victim lost control of his bowels before he expired. I didn't want to die with crap in my pants. An overdose of sleeping pills was the ideal way, but no one in my family used the prescription ones. And we had an electric oven, not gas, so I couldn't very well stick my head in it unless I planned on baking myself to death. That left me with slitting my wrists.

The more I thought about that method, the more appealing it became. If you did it in a warm bath, it wasn't supposed to hurt. I was in the middle of my ancient Rome phase, and the idea of bleeding to death in a warm bath seemed very Roman to me. Noble and quaint, somehow. And easy. The razor blades were right in the medicine cabinet and a tub full of hot water was just a turn of the faucet away.

The first suicide note I wrote was way too short. 'If I can't see Spencer any more, I don't want to live', it read, with absolutely no mention of Suey's meanness or Mom's neglect or Miss Lee's sudden stoniness. The second one rambled on for eight pages, front and back. A self-editor even at twelve, I tore it up and went back to the first one. I wouldn't even mention anyone else. Let them all wonder, I thought. Serves 'em right.

The matter of the note dispatched, I set about dispatching myself in the downstairs bathroom. I could use the blades out of Dad's razor and do it in the huge, claw-footed tub – if I had to go, at least my death would be stylish. But everybody used that bathroom. I wondered how long it'd take me to bleed to death. Mom was gone to her bridge club for the rest of the afternoon, and Dad would be at work for another three hours. I had no idea where Suey was. To hell with her.

I placed the note face up on my desk, weighted it down with my plastic monster models of Frankenstein and the Wolf-Man and went downstairs to finish the job. I passed by the phone nook at the foot of the stairs, thinking I ought to call Spencer and say goodbye, but Verna, the operator, had strict instructions not to place any of my calls. Miss Lee's influence in the town went far and wide.

I wondered if Spence was under the same kind of restrictions. Was he crying? Did he miss me as much as I did him? Maybe he was thinking about killing himself too. Maybe he was already dead and waiting for me. We'd read all about reincarnation. We probably wouldn't come back as neighbors, maybe not even as boys. It didn't matter. We'd find each other however we came back. I started crying again, like I'd been doing since they picked us up in Chicago.

I looked out the front window and saw Miss Lee in her rocker on the porch, rocking to and fro, her eyes trained on our house. I thought about going over to say goodbye to her, but I figured I'd get the usual silent treatment. That made me cry even harder. I loved Miss Lee more than anyone else in the world except Spencer, but that was over. She no longer loved me back. I should have put her name in the note, but I wasn't gonna go back and do it again. Crap.

I dried my eyes on the hem of my T-shirt, went into the downstairs bathroom and made sure I locked the door behind me. I found Dad's razor in the medicine cabinet. I couldn't figure how to get to the blade at first, but I finally popped it out. It fell into the sink and slid down the curve of the bowl, coming to rest against the stopper. The blade looked thin and fragile, but it cut my finger when I picked it up. It can't wait, I thought. It knows I'm doing the right thing.

I stuck the razor blade in the soap so I wouldn't lose it, then I got undressed, folding my clothes neatly and putting them on top of the toilet lid. The soft breeze from the open bathroom window ran invisible fingers over my naked skin, ruffling the few pubic hairs I had. My dick rose at its touch and I smiled. How could something that made me feel so good get me—get us—into so much trouble? I stretched my arms up to the sky, thinking it odd that I'd never felt more alive even though I was about to kill myself. And it didn't even change my mind.

I switched on the radio Mom kept on the windowsill, a cracked, tan plastic Zenith portable with makeup smeared across the speaker grill and a broken antenna pointing down towards the toilet. I turned the dial to CKLW out of Ontario.

Nothing left to do. No more preparations. Time to finish the job. The water still running, I climbed in the tub. The hot water bit my skin, but it felt good. I grabbed the bath salts Mom used whenever she was having one of her bad days and sprinkled some in the water, immediately wishing I hadn't. The room exploded with evergreen, like somebody crapped a Christmas tree.

The disc jockey's voice finally died out, replaced by a very familiar C/C7/B chord structure Spencer had been practicing on his guitar for weeks. It made me start crying again, and the tears came even harder when the Mamas and Papas started singing "California Dreaming". I could see him sitting cross legged in the treehouse in his frayed jeans and fringed leather jacket, his shaggy brown hair falling around his blue eyes as he strummed and sang, me doing my best to sound like Mama Cass to his John Phillips, echoing the words after him. We thought we had forever to learn it, but we'd never see each other again. That's when I reached for the razor blade.

Three little nicks. Two on my left wrist—one surface scratch for practice and then an inch long vertical stroke—and another cut on my right. None of that slashing across the wrist nonsense for me. I'd learned from Sylvia Plath that was for amateurs. And, yes, this twelve-year-old had read Sylvia Plath. Granted, I didn't get all the words or concepts, but I looked up what I didn't understand. She became my favorite writer despite the motherly librarian's best efforts to steer my poetic sensibilities into a "more positive" direction like Carl Sandburg or her personal favorite, Ogden Nash.

I folded the washrag into quarters and put it under my head for a pillow. Its damp warmth seeped into the back of my neck as my life seeped out of my wrists, the water now tinged a pinkish tone. I just settled back and listened to the radio. After the Mamas and the Papas came a Bob Dylan song I'd never heard before, something about visions of Johanna. He was Spencer's absolute favorite after the Beatles.

The water was very red now. My head was spinning. I felt

like I was floating above myself, floating above the tub, the bathroom, the house and everything else. I was flying toward the sun, toward a great big ball of light somewhere overhead, shining warm and comforting like Spencer's hand on my cheek. A roaring sound slowly entered my consciousness, the rushing noise of space and time drawing to a converging point somewhere in the distance, pulling me along with it.

Then I heard someone faintly calling my name. I couldn't go back and answer it if I wanted to, and I didn't want to. I was rushing madly ahead on the wave of sound, immersed in its depths and powerless to struggle against its advance. Faces and scenes from my life washed over me in a speeding collage of confusing images, vivid yet indistinct: Spencer and me waiting for the bus to Chicago, and then sitting in the seat in front of him and that guy and Mom screaming at us in the police station and me telling her how much I hated her and Suey laughing at me and slugging my shoulder and then suddenly it all stopped.

And I was alone in the quiet dark for a long time.

The beeping in my ears told me I wasn't in Heaven, unless the afterlife was noisier and more annoying than the life I'd just left. The restraints chafed my wrists, confirming my suspicions. I couldn't scratch my eyes. My eyes itched so much I had to open them, but I didn't want to. I knew I was probably in a hospital room. I had failed, and I was in shit so deep I might never see the top again. But my eyes itched. I had to open them.

I couldn't focus at first, but it got better as the beeping got fainter, as if bringing another sense to life lifted the burden on the rest. Something stood over me and spoke, but I still couldn't hear it over the beeps. It grew stronger in my ear, and I knew it was Spencer before I really saw him.

His grin, his long nose, his chipped front tooth, the tiny white scar under his ear from a rock I'd thrown at him during a fight, his blue eyes blazing down at me in relief, love, anger, and amazement. We never spoke much in those days. We said it all with our eyes. He lurched toward me and threw his arms around my neck, my restraints preventing a return hug.

His chest sank into mine like the last stone of a bridge between my halves. Filled with breathy heaves, he held me so tight it seemed we might teeter on each other's edges forever before falling back safely. We did fall back, though. Into a hospital room with the curtains drawn, facing a mean reality of hurdles, stumbling blocks, and people who couldn't understand. But we were together again. And that made it all bearable.

"How did you get in here?" I croaked. "Aren't you grounded?"

"Shirley passed out. Again. I crawled in through the window—lucky thing this is an old hospital and you're on the first floor in the back. I've been hiding in the bathroom in case someone comes in. You okay?"

I shrugged as he unbuckled the restraints holding my wrists.

"You scared the holy shit outta me," he said, freeing my right arm. I immediately reached up and rubbed my eye. "You gotta promise you won't ever do this again," he said in the most serious tone I'd ever heard from him. "Ever. I mean, you're all I have. You're the only thing that makes me want to get up in the morning. If you killed yourself, I'd have to do it too. And it kinda hurts that you wanted to leave me like that."

"I didn't. I didn't want to leave you, but I was so…ah Jesus, I don't know what I was. I thought about not seeing you again or Shirley takin' you away, and…fuck, I know it was stupid. I didn't think about…oh, goddammit, I'm sorry…"

He'd freed my left arm, and I sat up and hugged him harder than I'd ever hugged him before. "I love you," he whispered in my ear, "and I won't ever let you go."

I wanted to freeze that moment forever—put it in storage to take out and re-run whenever I felt like nothing was worthwhile anymore. Because I knew it wouldn't last. Moments like that never do. Familiar voices came from the other side of the door, outside in the hall. I recognized their timbre and their rage. Mom and Miss Lee were screaming at other. I couldn't hear the details, but I knew it wasn't good. It never was. And then the knob turned.

The door opened a crack, and Miss Lee paused, looking back over her shoulder. "I don't give a good goddamn what you or anybody else thinks, Bernice. This is between that boy and me, and I'm going in there and talk to him—alone."

Spence must not have heard, or if he did, he didn't care. We both held on to each other as Miss Lee came in. At the sight of Spence, her eyebrows flew up so fast I remember thinking they'd knock her tasteful black hat right off. She shut the door firmly behind her and locked it.

"Shirley must be passed out again," she said to him.

"Yes, ma'am."

"I'm not even going to ask you how you got in here because I don't want to know," she said, sitting in the uncomfortable look-ing chair next to the nightstand. Spence settled at the foot of the bed, crossing his legs. "I'm actually glad you're here. It'll save me a fight with Shirley. I don't want to see her any more than she wants to see me, but I have a few things to tell you boys."

I started to say something. I wanted to explain. I wanted to say I was sorry, both for Chicago and for trying to kill myself. I wanted her to know why. I wanted her to hold me—us—and tell us it'd all be okay, but she only held up her finger for silence. I stared at that knobby digit with the red nail and hushed.

"What you did was wrong, Kent," she said, "and it hits closer to home than you could possibly know. You boys...affect me. Now's not the time or place to explain it. Maybe I'll never be able to explain it. Your mother blames me for this whole mess, and I'm not so sure she's wrong."

I sat up. "But—"

Up came the finger again. "Not a word. Not until I'm fin-ished." She stood up and began to pace. "I'm going to close up the big house and go away for a while. At least six months, may-be more. I need to think about my part in all of this. And you two need to do some thinking yourselves. None of us can just close our eyes and pretend this never happened. It's gone too far and done too much damage already."

"To who?" Spence said, his voice strong and fearless. He always spoke when I couldn't.

"To me, young man. And to us." She gestured around to all three of us as she stopped pacing and drew close to the bed. "You stole fifteen hundred dollars from me. And don't tell me you'll pay it back because that's not the damn point. When you opened that drawer and stole from me, you stabbed a lifetime's worth of trust right in the heart. You killed something I cherished, and I did not deserve that. I have always fought for you boys and never regretted a single battle. Until now."

His fearlessness was gone. I could see the tears forming in his eyes as I felt them in my own. Miss Lee's tears were all in her voice. "Now," she said softly, "I don't know what's right any more. That's why I have to go away. I need to think about how to go on. And you need to think about that, too. I may be able to forgive you, but I don't know how I can forget." She edged closer to the door.

"Goodbye, boys," she said. Spencer started to move off the bed, but the finger came up for the last time. "Do not come a step closer, Spencer Michalek. No hugs. I couldn't bear hugs right now. But if you're smart, you'll leave the same way you got in here. Once I walk out that door, the parade will start. You don't want to be here for that."

He moved toward the window, sobbing openly if quietly. We looked at each other for a moment, then he clambered over the sill and dropped to the ground. The last I saw of his face was a red, tear-streaked mess that disappeared with a soft thud.

"Be good for your mother," Miss Lee said as she turned and left.

I never felt worse in my whole life. And I had no hope things would get better.

SENIOR PROM FOR A MOB

May 15, 1974

Are you *nuts?*" I said to Spence under my breath. "Go to Senior Prom together?"

Our homeroom teacher, Miss Vinson, stopped reading the announcements and glared at us. "Something wrong, boys?" she asked, scratching under her greying bun with a pencil.

"No ma'am," Spence said. "Just making plans for prom. How much did you say those tickets were?"

"Fifteen dollars single, twenty-five for a couple." She smirked and tucked the pencil back behind her ear. "May I ask who you're planning on taking?"

He jerked a thumb my way. "Kent."

We heard the usual "fags" among the giggles. "I think Mr. Carstairs might have something to say about that," she replied with an indulgent smile before moving on to the details of a Drama Club fundraiser.

"Why not?" he said a few minutes later as we got our first period books from our lockers. "We haven't been to one prom ever. This is going to be our last chance."

"They're not gonna let us go, Spence."

"Who? Carstairs? What's he gonna do? Get the police to keep us from coming in? We're students here, our folks pay the same taxes as everyone else's. We've got a right to attend our own senior prom." He stopped and looked in my eyes. "Unless you don't want to go with me."

I sighed. "It's not that. I'd be proud to go with you, but…"

"But what?" he said. "But they'll hate us? Make fun of us? They already do, Kent. Let's give 'em a reason." He smiled at me, and the matter was settled. I'd follow him wherever he wanted to go, including senior prom. But I knew what the reaction would be at home later on. Suey rolled her eyes and Mom slammed the bowl of mashed potatoes down on the dining room table so hard the water glasses rattled.

"Honestly, Kent," she said as she sat down, "do you stay awake nights thinking of ways to humiliate this family?"

"Everybody's talking about it," Suey added, forking the rarest piece of roast beef onto her plate. She knew I liked it rare.

"Nobody knows about it yet," I said. "We haven't even bought the tickets."

"I should hope not," Mom said, looking over at Miss Lee who was spooning peas into a little bowl. After Chicago and the botched suicide, Miss Lee had gone to Europe for a year, maintaining total radio silence for six months before she started sending us short letters at first, then longer and longer. We covered a lot of ground in that correspondence. Then, Dad divorced Mom, and Miss Lee came home. She'd eaten dinner with us almost every night since then. "I suppose you're all for this since it was Kent's idea."

Miss Lee smiled and handed off the peas to me. "I don't

think it was Kent's idea, exactly. Was it, Kent?"

"No ma'am."

"Doesn't matter whose idea it was," Suey said. "I still won't be able to get a date for prom, and it'll be their fault."

Miss Lee glared at her. "If you don't get a date for the dance, young lady, I expect it'll be because of your sour disposition rather than anything Kent might or might not do."

Mom's fork clattered to her plate. "*Mother*," she warned, "we've discussed this before."

"I know," Miss Lee said wearily, "but I won't sit here and listen to Kent be blamed for something that hasn't even happened yet. That's not fair either."

Mom sighed and put her head down. "Apologize to your brother."

"I won't."

She raised her head and looked Suey in the eye, daring a challenge. "You *will*."

Suey searched for support and found none. Her face and neck turned red, and she scooted her chair away from the table, balling up her napkin and throwing it at her plate. She hit her water glass instead, which spilled into the mashed potatoes. "I won't," she sobbed, running off to her room.

"Lovely," Mom said. "Just another quiet dinner." She got up from the table and followed Suey.

Miss Lee ate quietly. I took the piece of roast beef from Suey's plate and put it on my own, following Miss Lee's lead. At length, she put her fork down and fixed me in her gaze. "You're always testing things, aren't you?" she said. "You and Spencer."

"It's not that. We just want the same chance everyone else

has. Why shouldn't we be able to go to the dance together? All the other couples do."

"In a perfect world, you should. But this isn't a perfect world, Kent. People aren't going to like this. They'll think you're making fun of them, and they're going to fight back like they never have before. I hope you two have thought of that."

"As long as Spence and I have each other, it doesn't matter."

Miss Lee smiled. "I hope for your sakes you're as indestructible as you think love makes you. I'll tell you what, Kent. You go ahead and buy your tickets. Let me study on what might happen next. Maybe I'll even take a trip down to Denver and talk to Mr. Lee's lawyer. There might be more than one way to skin this cat. Now, eat your dinner before it gets cold."

That night, I heard Mom and Miss Lee talking downstairs, but I couldn't make out any of the words distinctly. I got out of bed and crept to the landing where I could hear better.

"...your aunt Charlotte," Miss Lee said.

"What does your dead sister have to do with anything?"

"It was the way she died."

"Gram said she died from cholera."

"Not unless she got cholera from the end of a rope."

"What? What are you talking about?"

Miss Lee sighed. "Charlotte was...like Kent. Even when she was a little girl, she said she'd never marry a man. She wanted to marry her best friend, Jenny. They used to have mock weddings in our backyard. Oh, everyone thought it was all kinds of cute, but I always knew Charlotte was serious. It wasn't until your Gram caught them in the basement doing things to each other that they finally realized the truth."

"What happened?"

"Jenny was sent away—the girls had to be at least fifteen or sixteen, because I was almost eighteen—but Charlotte was promised to a Mr. Nevins, a friend of father's, who had asked for her hand a year before. Lord, you should have heard the wailing when they told her she'd be marrying Mr. Nevins. She said she'd never live to see that wedding day."

"Oh, no..."

Miss Lee nodded. "The next morning, the whole house woke to mother's screams. Charlotte had knotted her bedsheets together, threw them over the rafter and hanged herself. I can still see her face some nights. Kent can't help what he is any more than Charlotte could. That's why I couldn't stay away even after they stole from me. It's the boy's life I'm thinking about. A gay son is better than a dead one, Bernice."

Mom didn't say anything for a long time. "Maybe. Maybe not."

I felt my stomach flip over.

"What an awful thing to say."

"Well, what kind of life is that, anyway? People hating you, making fun of you; the abuse he must take. All for that boy. It's just not right. And this prom thing will be a disaster, you'll see."

"Maybe if you were more understanding—"

"That's what he has *you* for. He doesn't trust me. And I can't figure out who he is or how to deal with it anymore, especially since Dan left. If that's selfish or cold or whatever, then that's how it is."

I couldn't listen to her go on. I went back to bed, but sleep did not come for a long time. I was thinking about Miss Lee's sister, Charlotte. Even though she was dead, by her own hand no less, the thought we had someone else in the family like me made me feel as if I wasn't an aberration. There had to be more somewhere in the family line. They may not have acted out their feelings or ever expressed them to anyone, but they had them. I was not alone, despite the fact that my own mother thought I might be better off dead.

And that really wasn't shocking after all. She'd already told me in a thousand small ways. Hearing the words was difficult, but I had Spence and Miss Lee, so love and support were in my life. I didn't need my mother because deep down I knew I never really had her.

Spence bought our tickets the next morning from a very surprised Margie Green, who sold them to us with a dazed, anxious look on her face. Her best friends Kim Norton and Janet DuPrie were also at the makeshift booth in the cafeteria, so our intentions were all over school by third period. By lunch, Mr. Carstairs had us in his office.

He entwined his fingers and put his palms together, making a ball that he held up to his mouth as he stared at us across his desk like he'd never really seen us before. Maybe he hadn't. He had no choice now. "Let me be frank with you boys," he said. "We simply can't have two male students attending prom as a couple. Now, I've heard rumors about you two being…well, you know…"

"Gay?" Spence suggested. "Queers? Faggots? Homos?"

He closed his eyes and rubbed his forehead as if in pain, his bushy eyebrows flattening out under his palm. "Whatever it is you want to call yourselves. And it's none of my business what you do or don't do off school grounds, but I'll tell you right now, this isn't San Francisco. The school board won't have it, and I won't have it."

"We're seniors," I said, "and our parents pay the same taxes everybody else's does, so we're entitled to the same rights and privileges as the rest of the seniors."

"That includes the prom," Spence added.

"You are perfectly free to attend prom," Mr. Carstairs said, "provided you bring female dates. But you may not attend as a couple. Do I make myself clear?"

Spence shifted forward in his seat and took a deep breath, but I put my hand on his arm and shook my head. He gave me a surprised look and backed off. "As clear as glass, sir," I said. "May we go now?" He waved us out of his office, turning the back of his big leather chair to us as he faced the window.

"Why'd you stop me?" Spence asked once we were out in the hall.

"He's not gonna listen to us."

"So, we're just gonna roll over and play dead?"

"Nope," I said. "Miss Lee said she'd help us."

Spence clutched the tickets in his hand. "Do you think she can do anything about this?"

"If anyone can, it's Miss Lee."

Miss Lee worked the phones for a solid week, cajoling, strong-arming, and threatening legal action. She even appeared at a special meeting of the school board along with Mister Lee's lawyer, who advised them our case was more than adequately covered by free speech protections. Gay couples going to school dances hadn't been specifically ruled on, but it was only a matter of time and the right court case. He also told them he'd be pleased to take this one as far as he could. "It'll be expensive and high profile in ways you probably don't want," he said.

In the end, the board and Mr. Carstairs backed down. Prom would be held, and we would be allowed to attend. Our victory was covered by the local press, which proved to be our undoing. The story got picked up by the *Denver Post* and the wire services, and then it went national. As it grew, it came to the attention of Anita Friebus of the Founder's Focus Group in Colorado Springs, a conservative Christian watchdog organization looking to branch out from anti-pornography campaigns and protesting X-rated movie theatres.

"This abomination must be stopped," she said on the local television news, a mic shoved in front of her pursed lips as she pushed her oversized glasses up on her nose and patted her not-found-in-nature blond hair. "It makes a mockery of the finest high school traditions, and we cannot stand idly by and see such perversion take place. Our Christian overtures have already been rebuffed by the Coyote County School Board, so we have no alternative but to plan our own assault on this travesty."

Miss Lee snorted as she snapped off the TV. "Travesty, my Aunt Fanny," she said. "That old biddy needs her ears boxed." The phone rang before she could sit down. "Oh, I'm not listening to that for two weeks," she said, glaring at it.

She marched over and yanked on the cord. It held the first time, but she wrapped it around her fist and gave another tug, pulling it free along with some chunks of plaster. A little cloud of dust rose lazily in the air as she smiled. "How about a nice piece of cherry pie, boys?"

But it would take more than cherry pie to get us through the two weeks until prom. In fact, reporters from the Denver stations and papers were waiting for us on the school steps the next morning. One was already interviewing Mr. Carstairs at the door. He could have just let us go in without pointing us out, but he stopped the reporter mid-question. "Here are the fellows you need to talk to," he said. "They're the ones going to prom together." Then the bastard slipped inside the building. I've always hated him for that.

They swarmed us with questions and demands, cameras and mics poking us from all directions. I was shaky, but I looked the red light straight in the eye and answered as best as I knew how—and the more I spoke, the easier it got. Spence took to the attention right away, already speaking as if he was a public figure. "We're doing this for ourselves," I heard him say, "but we're also doing it for gay kids everywhere who want the same rights as everyone else."

Reporters followed us all over town for a couple of days, but we thought it'd all blow over. It didn't. More and more of them came, prompted by Friebus's comments on rights.

"You can't grant rights for perversions," she insisted from the Founder's Focus Group's headquarters, which looked suspiciously like someone's front porch. "If this is allowed to spread, pretty soon we'll have students attending dances in the company of goats." She gave the camera a wink. "But I hear they're rotten dancers."

People came from everywhere, and they all needed lodging. You couldn't find an empty hotel room in a seventy-five-mile radius. Some townspeople took to renting spare rooms out in their houses. It was a regular boom-town atmosphere right up until the day of the dance. That's when things turned ugly.

Early that morning, two busloads of Founder's Focus protesters rolled up and settled in the Coyote High School parking lot, spreading out to make signs until Mr. Carstairs called the sheriff's department, who escorted them across the street to public property and established a presence to make sure they stayed there. They made their signs, marched, waved at passers-by and handed out literature, causing any number of pedestrian jams and traffic snarls. Reporters from in and out of state clogged Roberta's Café and Meecham's, drinking coffee and waiting for something to happen.

As stuffed as the town was, more people kept coming all day long, many of them finding their way to the access road up the mountain, blocking it despite the private property signs. Miss Lee kept the sheriff hopping that day, especially when she threatened to go down there with a shotgun and clear it herself. At one o'clock, Spence and I got called to Mr. Carstairs's office. When we got there, mom was waiting for us. She even had on jeans.

"Your grandmother and I thought it might be too risky coming home after school on the bus, so I'm running you home now." Gathering her yellow sweater around her, she looked at Spence. "You too. I've got the Jeep parked out back, so let's get going. You boys duck down as we pass those buses across the street. We'll be taking the other road up the mountain, so be prepared for a bumpy ride." She turned to go and spoke over her shoulder. "In more ways than one."

We drove the back streets through town until we came to

the access road cutoff on 127-A. Sure enough, about ten vans with dishes on their roofs lined both sides of the highway, reporters jockeying for the most scenic places to film their spots. Spence and I ducked down as we passed them and roared up the back road about a half mile out of sight.

We hung on to the seat and each other for the ten terrifying minutes it took to get up the side of the mountain. Mom wasn't an excellent driver, but she was a "gunner," meaning whenever she encountered an obstacle, she gunned the engine and drove over it. Thankfully, the Jeep tires were big and could handle most anything we encountered.

Miss Lee met us in the driveway with her cocked Remington over her shoulder. "Glad it's you," she said as we got out and dusted off our clothes. "I didn't think any of those reporters would be stupid enough to drive up here, but you never can tell. C'mon in. I tried to get hold of your mother, Spencer, but I didn't get any answer. You have your tux here anyway, right?"

"Yes'm."

"Good, because I'd hate to have to see what Mister Lee had that might fit you. Bernice, where's Suey?"

"Home since ten this morning. I brought her first."

"Well, then," Miss Lee said, breaking into a smile, "everyone's on the mountain that should be, except for those damn reporters. When do you boys have to leave for the dance?"

"Dance starts at seven, so I guess about six-thirty," I ventured.

"Good," she replied. "That gives me plenty of time to get supper going. Maybe even a chocolate cake if I get right to it." She handed me her shotgun. "Here, Kent. You stand guard. If any of those reporters shows his face, squeeze a shot or two off. Aim high. Make sure you miss, but put a good scare into 'em." She turned back and went into the big house, pausing at the doorstep for last minute instructions. "And give Spencer a turn too." The door shut behind her.

Mom shook her head and started for our place. "I hate this."

Miss Lee's supper was as good as her word: crispy fried chicken, mashed potatoes with lots of butter and cream, peas and triple-layer chocolate cake for dessert. Mom and Suey both had sick headaches and declined to join us for dinner, but mom said she'd have Suey ready for the dance by quarter after. She'd been able to find a date after all, but because of the reporters, they decided to meet at the school.

We got dressed after dinner, and Miss Lee got out the Brownie to take pictures of us holding hands by the fireplace in the library, then a few by the picture window against the sunset. As the colors faded and the sky grew dark, so did our mood. Spence grew quiet, and I couldn't help feeling a sense of dread and resentment. After all, this was supposed to be fun.

Miss Lee smiled and acted excited, but her eyes were tense and narrowed, and we knew she was more anxious than anything else. Mom and Suey were in the parlor when we came downstairs. Miss Lee still had her Brownie, but Suey didn't want to have her picture taken despite looking pretty good in a nice blue formal that set off her eyes. "I just want to get this whole night over with," she said, fussing with the back of her hairdo.

"It's not too late to stay home," Mom said. "This doesn't have to happen."

For a brief second, I almost took the out she'd tossed me. I could feel everyone watching me, but I couldn't back down. My gaze went from the floor up to my mom's, and for maybe the first time ever, I saw caring. I saw compassion. I saw what other kids must see every time they look into their mother's eyes. I wanted to save that moment forever, but I couldn't.

"It's too important," I replied, my heart sinking as that look on her face flickered out. Spence grinned and put his arm in mind. Mom sighed and turned away, either disappointed or revolted. Probably both.

Miss Lee headed for the coat rack in the entry hall. "Let's go, then," she said, shrugging into her long, black cloth coat.

"Are you driving?" said Mom.

"I am," Miss Lee replied, "and I'm taking the Eldorado down the front road, too. I'm not going to sneak down the back way like we're doing something wrong. Let's go, kids."

We filed past her, and all three of us got in the back of the Eldorado. Miss Lee paused in the doorway to say something we couldn't hear to Mom, then she fumbled in her purse for the keys as Mom stood in the door, gathering her yellow sweater around her. She actually looked worried. Not worried enough to go, but worried enough to frown with disapproval. That was a lot for her.

"Hang on," Miss Lee said, starting up the car and slamming it into gear. She peeled out of the driveway, throwing gravel everywhere as she headed down the side of the mountain. Gravity accelerated us as the heavy car barreled past trees, the occasional branch or stand of overgrown scrub brush scaping its side. Miss Lee braked some and we slowed a bit, but we were still hurtling down way too fast for comfort.

"Jesus Christ," Suey said under her breath.

"They won't be sticking their microphones in *our* faces," Miss Lee said by way of explanation. "They'll be too busy ducking for cover." She kept judiciously applying the brake, barely keeping the car under control, her mouth set in a tense line of concentration as she looped the steering wheel around to miss a boulder at the joint of a switchback.

Most people would have tried to stop or slow the car, but not Miss Lee. She wanted to see the intruders on her mountain panic as she approached, and she had faith that the Almighty would see us safely accomplish that goal. Somewhat less confident, we were too terrified to do anything but grasp the seat with quiet, white-knuckled fear.

The last half-mile came into view all too quickly: a straightaway half-illuminated by two streetlights on either side of the entrance. Miss Lee got her wish as the reporters lingering in the road saw us rocketing toward them. They screamed and scattered like roaches, diving into the underbrush as we whizzed past. Miss Lee grinned, but her eyes grew wide as she realized the road—and a guardrail keeping us from a sheer drop on the other side—rapidly approached.

She slammed down on the brake and cut the wheel sharply, narrowly missing the nose of a news van parked too close to the entrance. We hit the road with screaming tires, but Miss Lee kept her grip steady as the car's rear end smashed into the guardrail with a metallic thud, knocking a good chunk of it into the valley below before fishtailing back onto the concrete.

"Jesus H. Christ," Suey said. "You almost killed us."

"Nonsense," Miss Lee said. "And you watch your language, young lady. Don't think I didn't hear you the first time, either."

We may have come down the mountain quickly, but the road clogged up with traffic once we got in town. Between the protesters, their sympathizers, our supporters, curious residents, gawking out-of-towners, and people actually trying to get somewhere, we couldn't even get up to the twenty-five mile an hour speed limit.

Luckily, Officer Mann, Coyote's only motorcycle cop, was directing traffic on the corner of Beech and Main. Miss Lee flagged him over, pointing at his motorcycle leaning against the drug store. "Jeff," she said, "would you mind very much getting us through this mess so I can get the boys to the dance?"

"Like they're the *only* ones going," Suey said.

He took off his cap and ran his fingers through his thinning sandy hair. "I dunno, Miss Lee," he said. "Let me radio the chief. We've got all four men working tonight." He must have received permission because he mounted his bike and kickstarted it into life, turning on the siren as he motioned Miss Lee to follow him.

In a few minutes, we reached the high school parking lot, the epicenter of the action. All the protesters were out of the Founder's Focus buses, carrying their signs and chanting something we couldn't hear in the car. "HOMOS GO HOME," Miss Lee read as we pulled into the lot right after Officer Mann. "NO PERVERTS AT PROM. ADAM AND EVE, NOT ADAM AND STEVE." She clucked her tongue. "Charming. Lock the doors."

The sign wavers parted for the motorcycle and siren, but the mob rightly figured such precautions would only be taken for the principal players in this drama. They surrounded both the car and the motorcycle. Angry, screaming faces butted up against the windows. Miss Lee couldn't accelerate because Officer Mann was right in front of her, so we were trapped. The car began to rock, the windows now crowded with flat palms threatening to push us over. Suey began to cry, and I wasn't far from it. Spence stared out the window, wide-eyed and disbelieving.

Just as the rocking became violent, the sirens and lights of all three of the town's patrol cars came into view. They displaced the crowd, parking on either side and in back of us as Officer Mann and Sheriff Harmon appeared at Miss Lee's window.

"We've got some Summit County boys coming, but they won't be here for a while," Sheriff Harmon said. "If we can get the kids out of the car and into the school, we'll be in good shape." He stuck his head in and spoke to us in the back. "Are you ready to give it a try?"

We'd started it, and we knew we had to go through with it no matter what happened next. "I want to go home," Suey cried. Her hair was disheveled, and her mascara and makeup were smeared with tears.

The sheriff pursed his lips. "When we go, get her in the back of one of the black and whites," he said to one of the other cops. "They won't bother her once they see us leave." The door opened, and Suey was hustled away. As much as I hated her, I hoped I'd see her again. Because I wasn't sure how this was going to turn out.

"I'm ready," Miss Lee said, reaching under the front seat and grabbing her Remington. "Cocked and ready."

"You ain't goin' nowhere with that," Sheriff Harmon said. "I got kids and cameras and the whole goddamn world watchin', and the last thing I need is you and that damn rifle."

"Damnation. I need to see those boys to the door, Clint. I promised."

"You can come along, but without the Remington. C'mon, make up your mind. We got to go now."

"Fine." She stuffed the shotgun back under the seat. "You boys ready?"

We nodded.

"Okay," the sheriff said, "everybody get out on this side. We'll surround you, then all you have to do is keep walking. No matter what happens, keep walking. Clear?"

We nodded again. I slid over to Spence's side, he unlocked the door and we got out, sending a roar up from the mob. "Are you scared?" he said into my ear.

"Yeah."

"Me too, but don't let 'em see it. That's what they want. Keep looking ahead. Look right the hell at 'em. Smile a little if you can. That kills 'em."

Smile? I could hardly breathe. "I love you," I said.

"I love you, too."

Miss Lee held out the sides of her coat. "Do you boys want to duck under here?"

"No, ma'am," Spence said.

She drew us close to her. "You boys…" Her voice cracked, then she cleared her throat. "Let's go."

Miss Lee put her arms around our shoulders, the police surrounded us, and we stepped away from the police cars into the abyss of the mob. The shouts became a roar as our tight knot shuffled forward. Sheriff Harmon in front exhorted the crowd to step back and keep away through his bullhorn, but his command was swallowed by the angry noise.

Hands clutched at us between the policemen's shoulders, Miss Lee waving her purse in the air and shouting back at them. Spence and I said nothing. His silence, I'm sure, was more intentional than mine. The fact that our attendance at a stupid school dance could be the object of this much hatred stunned me so fundamentally that I had no response. Those faces, contorted by Christian charity and self-righteousness, still flash in front of my eyes no matter what kind of crowd I'm in.

My terror notwithstanding, I knew Spence was right. The only way to fight it was to meet it head on, and that gave me the courage to look back at them. I stared into their hot, angry eyes and tried to make them see the living, breathing human being beneath all the scorn they were heaping on me. And I think I connected with a couple. At least I hoped I did.

But one woman—a girl, really, not much older than those dancing inside the gym—kept bobbing into my view. She had longish dark hair, too much eye makeup and wore a baggy red sweater. She carried a sign that read, "HOMOS GO TO HELL" in one hand, holding a baby in her other arm. The child slept peacefully despite its mother screaming "QUEERS!" at us with such force her cheeks reddened, obscuring the stands of pimples there.

I caught and held her eyes several times, trying to see what was beneath, but her shell was too hard. I wondered what had disappointed or hurt her so much it could ripen into this kind of hatred. I wondered how the baby was able to sleep so soundly. Was it drugged? Lulled to sleep by the roar of the crowd? Or, even scarier, had it been on so many of these protests that it was simply used to the noise? The possibilities still running through my mind, we reached the gym doors, which Sheriff Harmon flung open.

Our prom theme was "Time in a Bottle," from the Jim Croce song. The decorating committee had worked hard on the banners and streamers, raising funds by selling bottles for students to seal wishes inside. These were all piled on a table near the refreshment stand. One of those wishes should have been for a better turnout.

The band played dutifully, but only eight or nine couples were on the dance floor with just a few more gathered around the punch and cookies. Many parents had kept their kids at home, either in silent sympathy with the protesters or because they were afraid of the crowds. And we were constantly reminded of the group outside. They peered in through the windows, holding up their signs as the police car lights strobed red and blue on the walls of the gym

Sheriff Harmon put his hands on our shoulders. "Now that you're inside, I'll get back out there and deal with those people. I'll leave Officer Mann in here just in case."

"Thank you, Clint," Miss Lee said.

Spencer offered his hand, which the sheriff shook. "Thank you very much, sir."

He smiled for the first time since we'd seen him. "Just doing my job. I don't know if you boys are right or wrong, but nobody should have to be escorted to a school dance by the whole damn police force. It's not right. We'll do our best to keep things in order until our Summit County reinforcements get here. It's gonna be a long night." He tipped his cap and was gone.

"I'm a mite thirsty," Miss Lee said. "I'm going to get a glass of punch. You boys want anything?"

"No, ma'am," I said as she smiled and walked away. What did we want? We were here with each other at prom, which is what we'd worked for, what Miss Lee had twisted arms for, what we'd withstood all the attention and all the scorn for. But it seemed like a hollow victory. Was this what fighting for your rights got you?

The band stopped playing and the few couples on the floor scattered, except for Margie Green and Bobby Hotchkiss, who headed straight for us. "I hope you're satisfied," she said, her underarms jiggling as she gestured toward the sparse crowd. "This is a disaster." Her neck and shoulders were as red as the corsage on her pastel green formal. "Do you know how hard we worked on this? And for what? Goddammit."

"I oughta kick your ass," Bobby sneered.

"Try it," Spence replied, stepping up to him. "I didn't walk through that crowd to let you push me around in here."

"Boys!" Mr. Carstairs shouted from the refreshment table where he was talking to Miss Lee. "Is there a problem over there?" Bobby turned red and backed down, grabbing Margie's arm and steering her away.

Spence let out the breath he'd been holding as he watched them leave. "Is it always gonna be like this?" he said.

"Like what?"

"All I wanted to do was come to the dance and have a good

time. I wanted to be like everybody else, just for a night, that's all. I didn't know. I didn't want this." His bottom lip quivered slightly.

"You can't cry," I said to him as the band started up again. "If you cry, they win, and I'm not gonna let that happen. Not tonight. And we are not like them. We're better. Let's go." I grabbed his hand and led him to the dance floor. The song? I'll remember it for the rest of my life: "Close to You." I took him in my arms, leading the way Miss Lee showed me as we shuffled through our first ever slow dance together.

The other couples drifted off the floor, leaving us by ourselves, lost in each other and the moment as we swayed beneath the banners in the gym. Holding him in front of everyone felt so powerfully right that I thought my heart might burst. A tear trickled down my eye, and Spence snuffled into my shoulder. With a few shambling steps around the dance floor, we signaled to the world that we were together regardless of what anyone thought.

I was so enthralled by these feelings it was easy to ignore the "Faggot!" I heard as we danced by a knot of students. What I couldn't ignore was the cookie that hit me square in the ear or the punch glass that whizzed by us and shattered on the floor a few feet away.

"Who threw that?" I heard one of the sponsors say. I craned my neck and searched what little crowd there was, watching Miss Lee swing into action with her purse as someone tried to separate her from Margie Green. That's when all hell broke loose. The table with the punchbowl overturned and cookies, punch glasses and unidentifiable objects flew toward the sponsors and adults, more than a few being lobbed our way. People shouted and screamed. Something hit one of the wish bottles, and the whole display clattered to the floor.

The band threw down their instruments and retreated as we stopped dancing and stared at the whole spectacle, rooted to the spot with nothing to hide behind. Officer Mann bolted away from the door, yelling and trying to restore some order. And that's when the second wave of hell broke loose.

Seeing the officer in the middle of the room, the vanguard at the windows figured correctly the entrance was unguarded. Both double doors burst open, the roar from the newly energized mob filling the room. Everyone in the gym stopped fighting and stared in horror at the crowd pouring through the doors.

And in the first wave was the girl in the red sweater with the baby. In her rush to enter, she tripped over the threshold, and the child slipped out of her grip. She halted and let go of the sign, then the crowd hit her from behind, and the baby fell to the floor. She dropped to her knees to cover it, but the angle was wrong and she slid to the side. Then they were swallowed from sight by the onrush of people.

Officer Mann and Miss Lee ran toward us. "Get the hell out of here!" Officer Mann shouted. "Head for the back doors. We're right behind you." We did as he said, but we couldn't budge the door. "Out of the way!" he hollered, hitting it with all the momentum he had. It flew open, flipping the bench that had been blocking it from the outside.

As we escaped through the back doors, the sheriff drove up in a black and white. "Damn Summit County boys still haven't shown," he said as we got in. "We can't get to your car—I'll take you up the mountain."

"The baby!" Spence wailed. "She dropped it!" He buried his face in my chest and began to cry.

"What's he talking about?" the sheriff asked.

Miss Lee sighed. "I don't know, Clint, but it can't be good. Please take us home."

It wasn't good. The baby, a four-month-old girl, had been trampled to death by the crowd. Her mother was badly injured but still alive. Editorials and opinion pieces across the state and nation tried very hard not to blame us, but a lot of people around town—behind Miss Lee's back, of course—said the child would still be alive if it hadn't been for us. I thought about it for years until it struck me that blame was not the point. As clichéd as it is, we're headed for death from the second we're born. Some of us just get there sooner than others.

When I think of that night, what I remember most is not the protests, the destruction of property, our personal danger, or even the death of the baby. What I remember is how the band played slightly off key, how Spence felt in my arms as we danced, and how I started to hope we too could live our lives like everyone else.

The rest? The rest is the unwanted baggage that often gets grafted to some of our most beautiful—and even ordinary—memories. It's the catcalls you hear leaving a restaurant from your anniversary dinner. It's the epithet shouted from a passing car while you and your husband are out walking the dogs. It's the photographer who refuses to shoot your wedding or the baker who won't provide your cake. It's the one-step-forward-two-steps-back waltz counting off a halting rhythm of progress.

It's also why we can't stop that dance.

PAVANE FOR THREE DEAD
WOMEN

1977/1978/1995

Straight men never lasted long on the mountain. Mister Lee died young, buried beneath the mine that enabled him to buy the place, so he was untested, but both our father and Suey's husband, Jake, left without much warning. Our dad stuck around for a while, but I'm not sure Jake even moved in with Suey. Chris may have been a motel baby. But at least the fathers lived. The early mortality rate for mothers was pretty high, as if they were too bitter to flourish.

Spence's mother, Shirley, died first, a victim of alcohol, isolation, and whatever kept her addicted and apart. Neither of us wanted to miss classes for Shirley's funeral, but Miss Lee insisted. "I don't care how bad a mother she may have been," she said. "I won't have her going to her reward with no one to see her off." Spence shrugged, nodded, and helped me pack our Pinto for the four-hour trip south from Boulder to Coyote Valley.

Spence didn't say much during the drive. I turned off the tape deck, thinking any cassettes in the smoky brown plastic case we had in the console between us might be too upbeat for the occasion, but we weren't halfway to Denver before Spence was shuffling through them. Before long, Thelma Houston's "Don't Leave Me This Way" came blasting through the speakers, though we remained silent on the "aaaawwwwww, bay-bah" part.

"Y'know what the worst part is?" he asked.

"What?"

"People are going to expect me to act sad or angry or whatever, but I don't feel anything. Nothing at all. I wish I could. It'd be easier than explaining."

"Don't explain," I said. "You don't owe anybody anything." I reached into the console and came up with a pair of sunglasses. "Here, put these on. They'll make you look grief-stricken without having to look a single person in the eye. They do it all the time in Hollywood."

A grin lit up his face for the first time that day. He put them on, leaned over, and kissed me on the cheek. "I love you," he said. "Let's leave right after the funeral."

"Miss Lee will want us to stay."

"We can tell her we have exams or something."

"She won't believe us."

"Probably not," he agreed, "but she won't say anything."

And she didn't. Mostly. She drew a deep breath and gave us a short, approving nod. "At least you came to pay your respects," she said. "That's more than most folks around here figured you'd do."

"How much do I owe you for all this?" Spence asked, his open palm turned sideways toward his mother's bronze coffin upon straps, ready to be lowered into the grave. A few mourners like my mom, Suey, and some of Miss Lee's friends milled around waiting for the minister so the service could begin. Birds chirped, basking in the sun of a warm fall afternoon. "I'll pay you back, just like with college."

"Oh, you *will* pay me back for your education," she said. "I have no doubt of that. But not for this. Doesn't appear people have done much for Shirley in her life. At least I can see her out of it with a little dignity. Take off those dark glasses and look me in the eye when I'm talking to you, young man."

With the glimmer of a smirk, Spence did as he was told. They locked eyes for a few seconds and when Miss Lee had seen what she wanted to see, she also gave a slight smile. "You're a good boy, Spencer," she said, patting his arm. "No reason to hide what you feel. Or don't feel. It's nobody's business but yours and Shirley's. Not even mine. Now, put those silly things in your pocket and let's go bury your mother." She took his arm and walked him to the gravesite as the minister drove up. I followed behind, proud of them both. As we reached the casket, I drew up even with them and took Spence's other arm.

The service started, mom and Suey fidgeting impatiently as the minister issued his comforting platitudes. The few other people in attendance looked bored and distracted, except for one person I hadn't seen drive up—a man who stood off to the side, well away from everyone else.

He wore a blue suit with a red tie, and he listened attentively, smoothing down his greying brown hair as the breeze stirred it. He radiated a quiet acquiescence, as if he knew he didn't belong and was waiting for someone to call him on it. His sudden presence did not go unnoticed by everyone else. Their glances were furtive at first but grew bolder. I figured Miss Lee saw him because she never missed anything, but when Spence looked up, I felt him stiffen.

No one paid much attention to the minister, who mouthed bland sentiments that only showed he didn't really know Shirley. Otherwise, he wouldn't have characterized her as a doting mother with a loving son. He eventually wound down to a final verse and an amen, and the winch lowered Shirley into her grave with no visible effect on anyone except for the man.

He shook with soft sobs, using his sleeve to daub his watery blue eyes, eyes that seemed to be a diluted version of Spence's the more I looked at them. He had to be Spence's father. Spence tightened his grip on my hand, and I realized he'd come to the same conclusion.

Shirley safely down, the mourners, or, more properly, attendees, began falling away from the crowd and drifting toward their cars, but we remained rooted to our spot. Spence didn't move, and neither did the man. They stood staring at each other from a distance, both of them so obviously in their own heads that I wondered if they weren't communicating telepathically. Who would break down and speak first?

Naturally, Miss Lee piped up. "Spencer," she said, "is that your father?"

"I don't know. Probably. I've never met him."

"Aren't you going to go over and say hello?"

"No."

"For heaven's sake, why not?"

He took a long time to respond. "I don't need to anymore," he finally said. "What would we say to each other anyway?" He raised his hand in a simple gesture of hello, received a return wave along with a smile and a wink, and the man turned and walked away. "He understands."

Miss Lee clucked and shook her head. "I'm glad someone does." She let go of Spence's hand, got between us and put her arms on our shoulders as she walked us back to the car. "Do you two have time for a bit of lunch, or do you need to get back to Boulder?"

"We should probably get back," I said.

She nodded. "I'm proud of you boys. You should really go over and talk to your mother and sister before you leave, Kent."

"Yes'm."

"If you change your mind, I'll be at Meecham's." She hugged us both, got in the Eldorado and drove off.

"Let's just go," I said.

"Can't," Spence replied, pointing his thumb at my mom and Suey, who stood talking by Mom's car. Well, Mom was talking. Suey was nodding her head. "We promised Miss Lee."

"Okay, but let's make it quick."

"It's pitiful," she was saying as we approached. "I've never seen such a dismal turnout in my life. I mean, I had no use for Shirley myself, but surely the Women's Club or someone could have rounded up…oh, hello Kent. Spencer. Listen, I want to thank you boys for coming today. Spencer, I know it must have been difficult for you, but you did the right thing."

My jaw dropped. Not only was my mother talking to Spencer, she was complimenting him. Suey, however, said nothing. Her head turned away, she stared off in the distance over the roof of the car. Rarely lost for a response, Spence nodded and gave Mom a slight smile. But the surprises weren't over.

"I know I haven't been a model parent where you two are concerned." she said, gathering her omnipresent yellow sweater around her. I wasn't sure if she meant me and Suey or me and Spence. "But it would *kill* me to think you wouldn't even come to my funeral…well, you know what I mean." She even grinned weakly. We smiled with her, but Suey continued to look away, her jaw set and her mouth in a grim line. Was it my imagination or did Mom look a little pale? Thinner?

"Well, I suppose we'd better be getting home. Are you boys going to Meecham's with Miss Lee?"

"I think we're going to head back to Boulder," I said.

Mom leaned in for a quick peck on my cheek. The move was so unexpected I almost recoiled but caught myself at the last minute and let her kiss me. It felt like a stranger. She did not do the same to Spence, so the world had not slipped completely off its axis. Suey reinforced my sense of normalcy by shooting us a foul look as she marched around the car and got in the passenger side.

Less than two months later, Mom was dead from an aggressive cancer of the "female parts" as Miss Lee put it.

"She knew," Suey said to me as we stood by the casket in Roberts Brothers Funeral Home, looking down at her emaciated, waxen corpse. "She knew she was sick when Shirley died."

"Did you know? Did she tell you?" Waiting for Suey to answer, I heard the buzz of people behind us. The main viewing room was full. Shirley may not have been able to pack the house, but they turned out in droves for Mom. She wasn't that well liked, but everyone wanted to curry favor with Miss Lee.

They were there for her, or for their own best interests.

"She didn't tell me," Suey finally said, "but I knew something was wrong. She had all these mysterious doctor's appointments and she always looked tired. You'd have to be stupid not to figure it out."

"I'm sorry." I didn't know what else to say.

She turned her eyes to me instead of Mom. "Sorry?" she repeated, blinking. "Sorry for what? Are you really sorry she's dead, or are you sorry for leaving us behind to be with him?" I drew a breath to say something, but she wasn't finished. In fact, she was getting louder. "Never mind. I don't need you to be sorry. And she sure as hell doesn't care anymore."

I felt someone coming up behind us, and I knew it was Spence. "Is there a problem here?" he asked, putting a hand on my shoulder.

"No more than usual," Suey said.

"Look…" He didn't get a chance to finish before Miss Lee appeared.

"There will *not* be a scene over Bernice's casket with the whole damned town looking on," she announced in an angry whisper. Miss Lee hated scenes except when she caused them. "I simply won't have it. Do you three understand me? The minister is waiting to start, so let's all sit down and try to get through this without bloodshed." Chastened, we went back to our uncomfortably close seats. We were right up front next to Miss Lee and Suey, but I would have preferred sitting in the back.

Do ministers ever say anything worthwhile at funerals? Does anybody listen to them, or are they all caught up in their own thoughts, wishes, and regrets? As I looked around, everyone else seemed to have tuned him out. A couple of people nodded off, their heavy heads jerking them back awake every few seconds. I was almost there myself when the minister concluded with an amen and a request. "Is there anyone who would like to come up and share a few words about our sister, Bernice?"

I expected a few seconds of awkward silence then blessed release from the stuffy room, but Miss Lee stood up. "I would," she said, sweeping up to the front of the room amidst low murmuring from the crowd. Spence and I looked at each other in disbelief and even Suey tried to catch our eye. This wasn't like her at all.

Still, she stood up next to the minister, looking small and trim in her knee-length black dress with simple pearls, setting off her elegantly styled silver hair and tasteful black hat without veil. She held her audience in a steady gaze and spoke out clear and strong.

"I expect anyone who knew Bernice could tell you she was a strong-willed woman, strong-willed and single-minded. That came from me. And I respected her for it. I didn't always agree with her. Fact is, most times I didn't. But you always knew where you stood with her. Problem is, people like that are hard to like. Even harder to love." Her voice broke a little, but she cleared her throat and continued, her eyes taking on a distant aspect.

"You never know how your children will turn out," she mused. "Oh, you know how you want them to be, but you don't have the last word. And the more you talk, the less they'll listen, so don't let anybody give you credit or lay blame at your feet because nobody knows what you've tried. Nobody knows."

She fell silent then, gazing at a point above the heads of the crowd. She seemed to be searching for the exact moment when things had gone wrong; the failure that marked the point when all was lost for her and her daughter. Silent, disconcerting seconds ticked by before Miss Lee finally rejoined us in the same room.

She leveled her gaze at the mourners once again, but she seemed momentarily stunned and embarrassed. She'd shown too much. She'd given us too close a glimpse and was unsure how to make a graceful retreat. She nodded once to the minister and went back to her seat.

After a mercifully short homily, we all filed out and headed to our cars for the procession to the cemetery. Spence and Miss Lee and I all rode in Miss Lee's Eldorado. Suey rode in her own car. Miss Lee hadn't said one word since the funeral parlor, and her staring out the window wasn't conducive to conversation. I wanted to hug Miss Lee and tell her everything was okay, but I wasn't sure she'd appreciate such an empty gesture. Or maybe she would. As well as you know someone, you never know how they grieve.

The ride to the cemetery was short and the graveside service even shorter. Miss Lee and Spence and I and Suey all stood around the grave as they lowered her down. Suey broke down then, letting out a gasp and a short burst of tears. She was the only one who cried. When she had recovered, we all threw a handful of dirt into the grave and stood there for a moment silently as the other mourners fell away.

Suey started to say something to us but didn't. She turned and walked away, shaking her head. Miss Lee continued to stare into the grave, holding both our hands, until the last car had pulled away. She sighed once and looked up. "I can't do any more for her," she said to no one. "Take me home, boys."

Again, the ride in her Eldorado was silent. We drove up the mountain and pulled into the big circular driveway. Suey's Corolla was parked in front of the little house she had shared with mom, now hers alone. Miss Lee didn't even look over in that direction. "Do you boys need any money?" she said, opening her purse.

"No, ma'am," I replied. "We're fine."

She clasped it shut again. "You just let me know if you run short, hear?" She opened the door and scooted over to get out. "I'd ask you in, but…I'm just so tired. I doubt I'd be able to keep my eyes open long enough to be fit company."

"It's okay, Miss Lee," Spence said. "You go on in and get some rest. We'll be fine."

"I know you will. Thank you, boys. Just leave old Bessie here. I'll put her away later." We all got out, and she headed for the door while Spence and I went to our car. She waved to us and went inside. We could see her through the window in the door as she unpinned her hat and put it on the rack in the entry hall.

Anyone in town would have given you even money Miss Lee, being somewhere in her sixties, would become the third nail in the coffin, but Miss Lee had no intention of making anyone's predictions come true except her own. She and Suey settled into a routine of willful ignorance. They lived across the driveway from each other but only spoke at the holidays when we all gathered at Miss Lee's for Christmas.

And at those gatherings, their conversation would be mostly directed toward us rather than each other. Miss Lee might make the occasional inquiry about how Suey's second-hand thrift shop was doing, or Suey would casually ask after Miss Lee's health, but their relationship was fallow. Until Jake sowed his seed, so to speak.

Jake, a thin, pale-faced nineteen-year-old, hitched into Coyote offseason from Vail, intending to work some odd jobs until the snow fell again. One of those was sweeping up and stocking the shelves at Suey's store, The Locked Closet. Spence and I always wondered where that name came from.

Despite the twenty-year age difference, boss and employee bonded quickly. Several times a day from what Miss Lee said. "Every time I go in there, they're always busy in the back. I'm surprised she bothers to turn the OPEN sign on every morning." In a couple of months, Jake was gone and Suey was pregnant. I never figured Jake would last. He was the means to Suey's end, the vehicle by which she got what she wanted. A baby. New life on the mountain.

But that new life brought new friction. The silence preceding Christopher's birth had been broken in favor of head-butting over how to raise the boy. They scrapped, battled, and occasionally compromised for the next seventeen years. Suey won some skirmishes and Miss Lee took others, but their conflict was well worth it.

Every year when we gathered at Christmas, we saw their handiwork and approved. Chris was turning into a fine young man with a keen interest in art as well as a talent for it. He wanted to go to the Colorado Institute of Arts, but Suey wanted him to have a more rounded education and insisted he opt for a regular four-year liberal arts program. No one could disagree with that, and we all worked toward that goal. Two weeks before Chris was to graduate from Coyote High, Suey was diagnosed with stage IV breast cancer.

Never one to shy from a problem or challenge, one of her better qualities, she faced illness with a grim determination. But she wasn't determined to live. She wanted to be catalogued, her decline charted by Chris's sketches. At her request, he'd sketch her once a day. She'd pose differently each time, sometimes asking him to draw her entire body or just her torso, or she'd want him to focus on one body part. She spared nothing. Nothing was too intimate.

"It's *indecent*," Miss Lee told me over the phone. "I'm not saying you shouldn't expose the boy to the hardships in life, but she has him drawing her mastectomy scars, for goodness sake. You'd think there'd be some middle ground. It's simply not right. You just don't share some things. People don't understand that anymore. If it's grotesque, it's up for grabs."

I pinched the bridge of my nose. "Have you talked to her about it?"

"She keeps telling me it's between her and Chris."

"Well, it kind of is, you know," I said with a sigh.

"You're going to have to talk to her, and that's all there is to it."

"Me? What makes you think she'll listen to anything I say?"

"I don't care whether or not she listens to you. She'll do what she'll do, but I want her to know someone else is questioning it. Maybe she can even explain it to you. Now, call her and call me right back."

"Now?"

"Of course, now. She's dying, Kent. We don't have time to play games." She hung up.

Suey didn't seem surprised at my call. "What took you so long?"

"You have Miss Lee pretty stirred up," I said.

"It never takes much to stir her up when Chris is involved."

"Did you really have him draw your mastectomy scars?"

"From two different angles."

"Why?"

She sighed. "I can't believe you're asking that question."

"Huh?"

"Listen to your own online lectures from SUNY. You said—and I quote because I have it on a sticky note by my computer—'Experience plus imagination equals inspiration.'"

"So?" I couldn't remember saying that. I didn't disagree, I just couldn't remember saying it.

"I'm giving him an experience, Kent. Something he can use. Maybe not now, not truly. He doesn't have the skills yet, but that'll come. He can draw on those memories, those sights and sounds and smells, whenever he needs to whether he knows it or not. You did the same thing, little brother. The suicide attempt, the bus trip to Chicago, senior prom with Spence—those are the things in the well you draw from."

She took a deep breath and continued, her voice raspier. I could tell she was getting tired. "I'm done, Kent," she said. "I've not got much time left and nothing else to give him."

"Hey, wait. You listened to my online lectures?"

"All of them. The private lessons, too. I've read all your

books, your articles, your blog stuff. Did you think I wasn't interested?"

"You never said. You never gave any—"

"Kent," she interrupted. "When we were growing up, all you *got* was attention—from Mom, from Miss Lee, from Dad when he was still around, from school, from our friends, from Spence. I wasn't about to let you know you had mine too." I could hear her take a puff from her inhaler. "I should probably tell you how proud I am of you, but I'm having enough trouble keeping food down."

"And how does Chris feel about having this experience?"

She wheezed more than chuckled. "I'm glad you asked that. He wasn't too keen on the idea at first, but then I told him it came from one of your lectures. I explained it to him exactly like I did to you. And, of course, he thought it was genius and took it a hundred times more seriously."

"Really?"

"Oh, stop being coy, Kent. It doesn't suit you. That kid has such a case of hero worship, it's not funny. And why not? You and Spence are everything he wants at this point in his life—coupled, successful, and famous. You matter, and he wants to matter too. I suppose he could pick worse heroes to emulate."

"Who are you and what have you done with my sister?"

"I wised her up. I waited too long, though. Maybe we'll all do better the next time around, huh?" She coughed until she ran out of breath. I heard the rustle of fabric as she dropped the phone on the chair or bed or whatever, muffling the hacking. It went dead after a few seconds. She didn't call me back.

Suey lived another sixty-seven days from that phone call. I

wanted to come out with Spence and spend some time with her, but she saw little point to it. "It's too grisly," she said, close to the end. "I even told Chris he could stop sketching me if he wanted, but he's determined to see it through. I like that about him, just not right now." She wheezed and breathed. "I'm getting tired, little brother. Time for me to go. Enjoy the time you have with my son. I'm jealous of it, but you can probably give him more of what he needs." Those were her last words to me.

Suey had seen to most of the details herself from the short, non-denominational service to the vaguely bronze-looking mid-priced casket to the plot next to Bernice. I watched them lower her down, wishing we'd had more time since we put things right with each other. I'd changed and so had she. And now, she was going into the ground right next to our mother who could poison her all over again.

Chris and Miss Lee stood together, their arms linked. Miss Lee wore the same black dress she always wore to funerals, but she had chosen a hat with a veil this time. Chris had no such adornment. He faced the morning glare with no sunglasses, squinting ahead stoically and dry-eyed, dark blond and beautiful. He looked much older in his dark blue suit, but not old enough to overcome the boyishness of his face. I remembered being where he was, Miss Lee at one side and Spence at the other, seeing one life out as my own stretched before me.

I sniffled, but I didn't cry. I never cried at death. Spence put his arm around me, and I leaned into him as we had done so many times during so many funerals and services and memorials during the epidemic. We hadn't done it as frequently in recent years, but our attendance at these events is once again on the upswing, probably a function of getting older. Everyone around us seems to be dropping off.

And as always, we put on our somber suits and our dark glasses, comfort the loved ones, and mourn over the gravesite while we compose grocery lists in our heads or wonder if we need to get gas on the way home. Either that's how pervasive grief is, or it's how insistently our lives demand to be lived.

I kept seeing in my head an image of a ghostly figure in a billowing grey robe with an oversized hood that obscured its features. It held a square lamp aloft in one arm, its hoisted sleeve unfurling from the spirit's appendage as the light illuminated the surrounding greyness. It reminded me of a Gustave Doré woodcut I must have seen a hundred times, but no matter how much I google, I can't find it.

Then, with the suddenness of a dream, I saw three of the figures marching by in a slow, steady processional whose point of origin was as arcane as its destination. Their lanterns swayed slightly as they moved past without any apparent means of locomotion. I heard somber musical notes in the distance but couldn't fit them into any discernable melody. Then the figures vanished.

But I still saw them. They were etched into the rocks of the mountains to the east, burned into the scrub pine and floating in the clouds. They appeared to me everywhere, revealing their outlines in the pattern of the minister's tie, the herringbone of a mourner's jacket, and the pile of dirt beside the grave. The evergreens sang their dirge loudly enough for me to hear it for a few seconds, and then it was all gone.

Spence looked at me with that mixture of wonder and anxiety he gets when he knows I'm too far in my own head. "Are you okay?" he said to me as we lined up to toss handfuls of dirt into Suey's grave.

"I think so," I replied. "Yeah. I think so."

MERCEDES GENERAL

June 28, 1984

Spence pulled the fork out of his mouth and looked at Kevin, his eyebrows flying up like they never did when he ate *my* food. "Oh my God," he said. "It's delicious."

And it was. Between the rich, savory scent of pot roast and the baked cinnamon goodness of what smelled like Miss Lee's apple pie wafting up to my second-floor office earlier, I hadn't gotten much work done on chapter seven. Only Miss Lee wasn't in the kitchen. It was Kevin.

Up until yesterday, Kevin had been a homeless boy haunting an apartment in a burned-out building across the street. He reminded us of what might have happened to us if we'd actually gotten to Chicago when we were kids. Spence took care of him like you would a stray cat. He used our doorstep to leave Kevin meals from Zabar's or a little Italian place down the block, and pretty soon Kevin started leaving us money on the doorstep in return—spare change, a dollar now and then.

We didn't need it. Miss Lee had loaned us the money for the four-story UWS brownstone we were renovating, plus Spence had a paid apprenticeship with a fancy NYC architect, but we took it in and kept it in a box by the door. We knew we'd get a chance to give it back to him. This went on for a week, then one night I answered a knock on the door and there he was. We offered him a shower, a hot meal, and a sofa for the night. In turn, he offered to cook for us the next day.

"Told ya," Kevin said, finally taking off his apron and settling into one of the kitchen chairs. He pulled it up to the table. "There's plenty of mashed potatoes, and I got more ears of corn roasting in the oven, so dig in."

The meat was the most tender I'd ever tasted, and the gravy had an unidentifiable yet addictive tang. The potatoes were fluffy and buttery, and the corn on the cob was the best. Even Miss Lee didn't roast corn in the oven. I had to second Spence. "It's really, really wonderful. What's in the gravy?"

"Sour cream. So, do I get the job?"

"Was a job involved?" I said to Spence.

He smiled. "If there wasn't, maybe there should be."

"How old are you?" I asked.

"Ni—uh, eighteen."

"Eighteen?" I said. "*Really?*"

"Okay, seventeen and a half."

"Where are you from originally?" Spence asked.

"Los Angeles."

"Where did you learn to cook like that?"

"Los Angeles," he said, rolling his eyes and tossing back his sandy hair. "Look, my mom died when I was thirteen, but before that, she taught me a little. I cooked for my dad and brother after she died. To be honest, I can only cook a few things really good—roast, chili, spaghetti sauce, Thanksgiving turkey with all the trimmings, pork chops—I want to learn more, though.

Now, if I had a job, I could buy a coupla cookbooks…"

"We have cookbooks," I said.

"We do?" Spence said. "How come you don't use 'em?"

Kevin shook his head. "You probably have Caucasian Chili a lot—y'know, like last night?"

"Caucasian Chili?"

"Yeah, ground beef, canned beans, tomato sauce, maybe an onion and some chili powder for color."

"That's par for the course," Spence said.

"Okay, okay," I said to Spence, "I'm trying to write a book here, and I have enough distractions with contractors and drywallers and painters and whoever else is tearing shit out this week. I'm lucky if I have an outlet for the Selectric. You're busy with your apprenticeship, and I hate cooking."

I turned to Kevin. "So, here's the deal—seventy-five bucks a week, your own room, and a food budget. You do the shopping, the cooking, and the cleaning plus answer the door and the telephone."

Spence raised his eyebrows. "Shouldn't we talk about this first?"

"You just complained your way out of that discussion. What do you say, Hazel?"

"I say it's better than the burned-out building across the street, and don't call me Hazel."

"Fair enough. You *do* know we're gay, right?"

"Duh. So's my brother."

"How about you?"

"Me?" He shrugged, tossing his hair once again. "Hey, I've been homeless for a year and a half, so y'know... You gotta do

110

what you gotta do—does that mean I have to put out? Cause that's extra."

Behind all that bravado was a scared little boy who desperately wanted somewhere he could belong. And I thought of Spence and the pedo on the bus to Chicago, felt his shame and revulsion at what he'd had to do. He wouldn't let me kiss him for a couple of weeks after. Not even on the cheek.

I hoped I hadn't taken too long to answer. "No. No putting out."

"Wednesdays off?"

"I guess so," I said. "Why Wednesdays?"

"That's when they change the movies. Hey, you guys see *Conan* yet? Ahnold kicks ass!" he said, feinting with an invisible sword. "How about *Ghostbusters?* The new *Star Trek?*"

We shook our heads.

"Don't get out much, huh?"

"How does a homeless kid get into all these movies?" Spence asked. "Sneak in?"

"Naw, that'd be wrong. But if you blow the Wednesday ticket taker, he'll let you in for nothin'. Free popcorn and a Coke if you let him come in your mouth."

"There's a tip you won't read in the *Times,*" Spence said with a chuckle.

"Probably not even the *Post,*" I replied, extending my hand to Kevin. "So, do we have a deal?"

He smiled and shook. "Deal."

When Kevin wasn't reading cookbooks, he was plowing through Tolkein's *Lord of the Rings* trilogy he'd picked off our bookshelves. "Best book ever," he declared. In a couple of months, Kevin wasn't part of the household, he was *the* household. He rode herd over the workmen, allowing me time to write while he cleaned, answered the phone, and prepped meals.

After dinner one night, Spence grabbed the remote control as he sat down next to me, handing me a Diet Coke with ice. "*Love Boat* or *Bosom Buddies*?"

"Who's on *Love Boat*?" I asked.

He shook out the TV listings and put his glasses on. "Bert Convy, Patty Duke Astin, Arte Johnson, and Michelle Phillips."

"I think we saw that one. What's on CBS?"

"Football."

"Pass. Let's go with *Love Boat*."

"No *Bosom Buddies*?"

"They should leave drag to the professionals," I said as Spence switched channels and the *Love Boat* theme echoed through the room. "Besides, Tom Hanks gives me the creeps."

"Who gives you the creeps?" Kevin asked as he breezed into the TV room, taking off his checked apron and throwing it over the arm of the occasional chair. He sat down with a grunt.

"Tom Hanks—the tall one on *Bosom Buddies*," I said. "*Love Boat* okay?"

"I'll watch anything that isn't a burner on the stove."

"Speaking of which," Spence said. "If we didn't mention it, those scalloped potatoes were terrific. I've gained ten pounds, though. I may have to start running again."

"Do a mile for me," I said. "You're doing a great job, Kevin.

The place has never looked better, I'm up to chapter twenty, and the contractors are almost finished with the third floor and ready to start the fourth. I think they show up just for your chocolate chip cookies."

"Cut it out, guys—I'll start blushing." He grinned and tossed his hair, his go-to gesture whenever he ran out of words. "Seriously, thanks. That was my first try at scalloped potatoes. Next time, I'm gonna use some homemade stock instead of can—"

The phone rang.

"Sit, sit," he said, getting up and taking the apron with him. "I'll get it." He jogged out of the room to pick up the kitchen extension.

Spence rubbed my shoulder with his big hand. "I have to say, I had some doubts about this whole arrangement, but it seems to be working out pretty well. Good job, you."

"Sometimes you just have to go with your gut instincts."

"Michalek-Mortenson residence," we heard him answer. "*Riley?* Wait, wait, slow down…he did *what?*...why?...oh, shit. How did he find out?...*what?*...you're shittin' me…when did you get out…are you okay?"

We looked at each other in confusion waiting for more, but Kevin was silent for a few minutes. Spence started to say something, but I shushed him.

We couldn't make out what he said when he started talking again, but his voice broke a couple of times. "Look," he finally said. "Where are you?...Port Authority?...no, no, you did the right thing…I don't know, but I'll be there as quick as I can. You're gonna be okay, Riley. Trust me. I love you, man. Don't fuckin' move. Bye."

Spence and I heard him hang up the phone, then he appeared in the doorway, pale and obviously shaken. "Um...shit, I don't know where to start..."

"What's going on?" I asked. "Bad news?"

"Yeah. That was my brother, Riley. Dad kicked him out of the house. He's at the bus station, and he needs my help. How do you get to Port Authority? And can he stay here? He can bunk in with me, it's okay. He's...sick...and I...I...just don't know what else to do." The tossed hair again.

"God*dammit*," Spence said, "I fucking *hate* parents like that. Of course he can stay here. Don't worry about getting to the bus station—I'll drive you." Spence looked at me, and I nodded.

"Absolutely," I said. "He can stay in one of the third-floor bedrooms or we can put a cot in your room—whatever's easiest. He'll get back on his feet. It'll be okay."

Kevin's tears started flowing, and he sagged against the doorframe. "I don't think so. He has it."

"Has what?"

His silence said it all.

"Jesus Christ," Spence said, not pausing a moment. "I'll bring the car around."

Although the bus station at the Port Authority is big, finding Kevin's brother wasn't tough. After glancing around once, Kevin beelined for a bench surrounded by a bunch of security guards and cops. Spence jogged behind him, and I brought up the rear, knots forming in my stomach. Spence never mixed well with the police. Those knots tightened when I saw one of the uniforms kick the bench.

"*Hey!*" Spence bellowed from a good twelve feet away. All heads turned his way, Kevin taking advantage and diving between them toward his brother. "What the *hell* are you *doing?*"

The shortest, thickest cop levelled his angry gaze at Spence, hooking his thumbs in his belt and wrapping the rest of his right hand around his baton. The fluorescent lights shone off his bald head, and he was sweating round his thick neck. "Movin' this loitering faggot along if it's any of your business, mac."

"First of all, the name's Spencer and second, he's not loitering. He's waiting for some faggot friends to pick him up after a long bus trip from LA. That would be us. And if you kick that bench again, we're gonna have a fuckin' problem."

The cop's eyes widened, and he pushed his bulk against Spence, who remained immovable. "Looks like we got a fuckin' problem right now." Just as he started to raise his right hand and unsnap his baton, one of the other cops touched his shoulder.

"Leave it, Marty," he said, not even looking at Spence. "You don't wanna catch nothin'—besides, we gotta eat. Let's go."

They glared at each other for an uncomfortable moment, then Marty the Cop turned away without a word, and they all walked off, the peacemaker giving us a last-minute instruction over his shoulder. "Get him outta here."

I wasn't sure who he was talking to or about, but I was more than happy to comply. Spence was shaking, as he normally did after these encounters. I knew he'd have it together in a minute, so I turned my attention to Kevin and his brother half-sitting, half-lying on the bench. Kevin was kneeling, cradling Riley's oversized head in his hands as he whispered in his ear.

Riley's head wasn't bigger than normal; there just wasn't much to the rest of him. He was unshaven and smelled of medicine and bandages. His white, long sleeved button-down shirt and jeans hung on his emaciated frame, so skinny I don't know what kept him from falling between the slats of the bench. The dark Kaposi lesions on his arms and chest showed through the thin white shirt. His dark hair was patchy, and more seemed to be falling out every time he coughed. He had blue eyes like Kevin, but his were dull and rheumy.

I got on the other side and signaled Kevin to stand. "Let's get him on his feet and get out of here. Can you stand up?" I asked him.

"I…I think so," he said weakly.

"I'm Kent, and this is Spence. You're coming home with us."

"No…it's too—"

"It's not," I said. "Save your breath. I'm sure you're exhausted after that bus ride, so we're going to get you home and let you rest. You'll feel better soon, I promise. Where are your things?"

"Don't have any. I left from the…hospital."

"Fucker wouldn't even let him pack," Kevin said, tears in his voice.

Spence looked like he wanted to punch a wall.

"Don't worry," I said. "We can find something for him to wear. We'll take care of it. Okay, Riley, we're going to stand you up on three. Help if you can, but let us do the work. Ready, Kevin? One, two, three…"

It was like lifting a sack of bones. I could almost hear him clatter. Kevin and I walked him out of the Port Authority, Spence's helpless anger surrounding us like a protective bubble against the stares and whispers of those we passed. People pointedly stayed out of our way, and we got to the car without incident.

"It's the red Mercedes over there," I said to Riley as Spence dug out his key.

At first I thought he was coughing, but then I figured out the noise coming from his throat was a chuckle. "A *Mercedes?*" he said. "Look at you, brother mine—comin' up in the world."

Kevin smiled. "Yeah, but the neighborhood's so bad, we gotta park it in a garage down the block. Welcome to New York City."

Dr. Berkowitz took the stethoscope out of his ears and a pack of Pall-Malls out of his pocket. He lit one up and looked around the bedroom where we put Riley. "The place is coming together. What's this color?"

"Spanish Sandstone," I said. "What's the deal, Harvey?" Spence and Kevin were crowded anxiously around the other side of the bed. Riley's chest rattled as he breathed, his eyes opening and closing occasionally.

The doctor exhaled, waving his hand in the air to rearrange the smoke. "I imagine they told you in the hospital how sick you are, young man," he said to Riley, receiving a weak nod in reply. "It's called pneumocystis carinii pneumonia—PCP for short— and it's pretty common with—" He glanced up at Kevin then stopped. "You taking your clindamycin?"

He shook his head. "I...I...don't have any."

Harvey raised one eyebrow. "You can't get better if you don't take your meds."

"Look, the poor guy got kicked out of his house when he got sick," I said. "From what I understand, his dad had him discharged, and he went from the hospital to the bus station."

The doctor pursed his lips. "God, I hate people," he said. "I'll write the scrip. Call my office and talk to Nurse Ratched. Don't tell her I called her that. She's wicked mean, but she'll take care of it. Does he have any insurance?"

"We'll cover it."

"You can take it out of my salary," Kevin said. "Or I can owe you or something."

"We'll take care of it," Spence said. "We just need to get your brother on his feet."

Harvey raised the other eyebrow. "Your brother?" He sighed heavily and leaned down to Riley. "You just rest, my friend. You'll feel better once you have a few days of medicine under your belt. I'll check in with you then." He laid a hand on Riley's shoulder. "No bus trips, okay?"

Riley managed a faint smile. "I'll try."

The doctor stubbed his cigarette out in the ashtray on the nightstand, signaling for us all to leave. We went in the hall and Dr. Berkowitz closed the door behind him. "I hate this conversation," he said. "Young man…"

"Kevin."

"Kevin. We can manage the pneumonia and get him as healthy as possible, but this is not a curable condition. The trick is to avoid other opportunistic infections as his immune system—what keeps the rest of us healthy—is wiped out."

"How long does he have?" Kevin asked.

"I wish I could tell you. There's just so much we don't fucking *know* about this thing. I mean, we can't even test for it yet. All I can tell you is what I've seen over and over. It's not spread by casual contact. My colleagues and I think it's blood borne, meaning your blood has to come in contact with infected body fluids. That's why so many of the cases I've seen are in men who are receptive partners. I have to ask you a very personal question, Kevin."

"Shoot."

"Have you had anal sex?"

Kevin reddened. "Once."

"How long ago?"

"About a year. It...I mean, I...I was hungry. I didn't have any money for food and this guy, he—"

The doctor held his hand up. "I get the picture. I'll bet he didn't use a condom."

"A what?"

"A rubber," Spence said.

Kevin shook his head. "Do I have it?"

"Doubtful if it was just the once a year ago. You would have seen symptoms by now—weight loss, weakness, the dark lesions your brother has. My concern is keeping the rest of you healthy at this point. No sex without condoms. Understand?"

"Yes sir."

"And just so you two don't get smug, are you monogamous? Have you been all this time?"

"Yes," we both said.

"Good. Keep it that way. Don't cheat and lie—if you're going to cheat, tell the truth. I'd rather someone's feelings got hurt than either one of you die. Okay, rant over. Going to Fire Island for Halloween? Asa wants to, but I don't know."

"I'm not sure I can get away," Spence said. "Interns always get the shaft."

"Just make sure that's a figurative shaft," he said, facing Kevin and shaking his hand. "I'm sorry about your brother, son. We'll do the very best we can."

Kevin looked shell-shocked. He hadn't gotten much sleep but still managed breakfast, not that we'd eaten much of it. "Thanks, doc," he said. "You want some coffee to go?"

The bactrim and the corticosteroids worked better for Riley than the clindamycin did, but he was still mostly in bed, sleeping or reading Tolkein's *Lord of the Rings* trilogy, which Kevin had given him. Sometimes Kevin or I would read it aloud to him after dinner. However, he had a few good days when he was actually able to come to the table for breakfast, Kevin making wild plans for touristy NYC trips Riley would never be able to take. But he'd smile and nod as enthusiastically as called for.

Riley was always a question mark to me; a missed opportunity to understand who Kevin was. I could never fathom their relationship. If I walked into Riley's room during a conversation, they both clammed up. Maybe it was the dead mom or the angry dad, but they were a closed unit. I resented it at first, but then I saw how much Spence and I were like that, and it made more sense.

One morning when we walked into the kitchen, Riley was already sitting at the table with a plate of pancakes and sausage. Kevin was making more, having cut his usual X in Riley's stack, "so the syrup has someplace to go." But from the congealed mess on Riley's plate, they'd been sitting untouched for a while. His fork was in his hand, but his hand was dragging on the lap of his bathrobe. He watched Kevin, occasionally raising his cup of coffee for a shaky sip.

"Yeah, Staten Island is definitely too far," Kevin was saying, turning sausage patties with a fork as he looked over his shoulder at us. "Morning, guys," he said. "Just trying to figure what Riley might be able to do today. You got any ideas?"

Spence and I looked at each other, both of us stuttering and not really saying much of anything until Riley spoke up.

"I have an idea," he said, raising his hand and putting his fork back down on the table. He pushed away from the table, planted his cane on the floor, and slowly shuffled over to Kevin at the stove, almost catching his bedroom slipper in a hooked rug in front of the counter.

Kevin almost looked shocked as Riley advanced. He stopped turning the sausages. "Yeah?" he asked nervously. "What?"

Riley smiled weakly as he stopped in front of Kevin. "I was like this with Mom," he said. "You were too little to realize it, but every time she had a good day I'd be begging her to do stuff with us. And sometimes she would. Remember?"

"Sorta."

"Well, it cost her. She'd be extra sick for a couple days after,

121

so I finally figured out maybe if I didn't push her on her good days, she'd have more of them. You see what I'm sayin'?"

Kevin had his head down, nodding wordlessly as the sausages started smoking. He wiped his eyes on his apron and took the frying pan off the burner.

"I love you, Kev," Riley said, "but I'm not gonna make it through this. I'm not getting any better. I can feel it, so let's not spend this time ignoring stuff or pretending to each other. I'm gonna go back to bed for a while. Maybe when I get up, we can sit out on the stoop. But that's about all I'm gonna be able to manage." He kissed Kevin's forehead and turned away, waving to us as he left the kitchen.

We heard his soft, slow progress upstairs until the floorboards began to creak above us. Kevin started switching off burners with lightning speed. "I gotta take a walk," he said, grabbing his jacket from the back of a kitchen chair and heading for the back door. His sobs were audible for half a block. Spence reached across the table, took my hand, and we sat there for a moment quietly watching residual smoke rise from the half-burned sausages on the stove.

Then Riley got a roommate.

"His name's Rodolfo," Kevin said one night at the dinner table as he was clearing plates away. "We used to be homeless together. He's a solid guy. Just got over PCP, but he knew something was up and went to the doc right away. Didn't let it get too bad. But he lost a ton of weight, and the restaurant he works at found out he was sick and fired him. Now he can't pay for the room he rents. It'll just be temporary."

"How temporary?" I asked.

"A couple of weeks," he said, fixing a tray for Riley. "Maybe a month. Just to fatten him up a little bit so he can get a job. He can't get better sleepin' in the park. Look, I know you guys aren't made of money, and I owe y'all so much already. Riley's costing you a bundle..."

"Not so much," Spence said, though that wasn't quite true. Dr. Berkowitz wasn't charging us for stopping by when he could, but the drugs weren't cheap.

"And I can feed everybody with the budget I have, so we're good there. Roddy's quiet, so he won't bother your writing none. I'll move him in with Riley, and they can keep each other company."

I took the silverware and glasses over to the sink. "How much longer do the drywallers have on the fourth floor?"

"Four days. They said two, but I've seen 'em work. Then the painters next week, and the job's done." He grabbed a spoon and napkin from one of the drawers and scootched his head down to look at me. "So, can Roddy stay with us?"

"I don't know," I hedged. "I mean, Riley's family. Why don't you get him fed, and Spence and I can talk about it."

"Cool, thanks—banana cream pie's in the fridge. I want to read him a chapter or two of *The Two Towers* while he eats, so I'll be down later." He picked up the tray and went upstairs while I took out a couple of plates, a fork for myself, and a spoon for Spence.

"You should have just said yes," Spence said as I sat them

down and went back for the pie. "You know you can't resist strays."

"Me?" I brought the pie and a knife back to the table and cut two slices. "You're the one who started leaving Zabar's on the doorstep."

"I wouldn't have done it if I didn't think you'd go along with it." He took the bigger piece. "Besides, it's worked out. You can kiss the roof garden and the finished basement goodbye for right now, though."

"We still have money left, don't we?"

"Enough to fatten Rodolfo up," he said, licking whipped cream off his spoon. "We'll be okay."

"I just…I mean, it's getting bad out there. Berkowitz says he sees a couple of new cases a day. None of the docs he works with will even bother with them. They see the symptoms and just write the poor kids off. Minimal government funding for research—fucking Reagan can't even *say* the word—and these guys are dying every goddamn day. It's not right. Somebody ought to do something."

"I totally agree," Spence said. "That's why we should let Kevin's friend stay. As least two people will have some kind of refuge."

"That's not much."

"Look," he replied, scooping out the last of the pie filling with his spoon, "the only thing we can do is keep our corner clean and help where we can." He dumped his crust on my plate and kissed the top of my head as he took his dish to the sink. "Shall I tell him the good news and bring the car around while you get a cot out of the basement?"

"Sure," I said, mixing his crust with the rest of my filling. "But I'm finishing my pie first."

Roddy, a Latino boy with painfully beautiful brown eyes and a smile that took your breath away no matter how emaciated he looked, moved in that night. He was followed by a Black kid named Levon who worked in Spence's office until a secretary saw him coming out of the free clinic. His bosses asked some hard questions he answered fully and frankly before they fired him for poor performance and missing too much work even though he'd only been late a couple of times.

Around the time Levon came, we also took on Dr. Berkowitz's nephew, Allen, in partial payment for Harvey's increasingly longer visits. And Harvey brought us three of his patients: Theo, Steven, and Robert, who had the additional problem of a broken jaw his father had given him upon diagnosis. And that took care of the third floor, our strays all picked up and brought to the brownstone by Spence in his red Benz, leading Kevin to dub the place "Mercedes General." The boys pooled what meager funds they had—a few of them worked sporadically but most were too sick or had been fired for whatever bogus reasons their employers could concoct. They contributed what they could, but most of the money came from our building fund.

Kevin not only worked miracles with the food budget, but he morphed into a human dynamo with a seemingly inexhaustible capacity for patience, planning, cleaning, and counseling.

He had long ago stopped going to the movies on Wednesdays and refused every raise we tried to give him. "Put it on Riley's account," he insisted. "I got all I need."

But what neither he nor the rest of the guys had was family, so we became our own. Kevin always joked and mugged for the boys when he delivered meals and sometimes gave cooking tips to them when they'd come downstairs. "This'll come in handy when you're out on your own again," he'd say, always optimistic. Those who were ambulatory ate with us at the table, sharing bits of their stories and trying for a few minutes of normality. Allen would ask Harvey about his mother when he stopped by for rounds, receiving the same "She'll come around" every time. But she never did. He eventually stopped asking.

We also got a lot of aborted phone calls, confronted by angry silence or halting, nearly incoherent queries when we picked up the line. Lots of hang-ups, too. Sometimes, Spence and I could hear hushed, tearful conversations from the phone nook near the stairs late at night. We took to keeping a box of Kleenex there and left the answering machine on full time. Spence kept working at his internship and somehow, I got a first draft of *The Stranger Within* written, but after a few months, the unavoidable started happening.

Riley died before we could finish *The Return of the King*. I was reading to him while Kevin and Roddy were delivering trays to the other room, and I had just finished the passage where Gollum saves Frodo from the elf-soldier denizens of the Dead Marshes. Particularly proud of the emotion I was putting into the piece, I looked up at Riley for his reaction and noticed he wasn't breathing. I shook his shoulder gently, and his head fell lifelessly to the right.

He wasn't the first person we knew to die during the epidemic, but the rest had only been acquaintances. Friends of friends. This was one of our boys, and I couldn't help the dry sob that escaped me—especially when I realized the same fate would befall each of our charges when time and inevitability pulled them under the waters of their own Dead Marshes. And there wasn't a goddamned thing I could do about it except watch that murky pool spread.

The first three crematoriums we called wouldn't even take Riley's body once they found out the cause of death. The fourth one agreed, but the circumstances under which we were to deliver him were so furtive and clandestine it was comical. But no one was laughing. And when we picked up his cremains, we were cautioned by the owner not to be too forthcoming about their involvement as he didn't want them to be known as "the AIDS crematorium."

"Fuckers," Kevin said in the backseat, clutching the box of ashes. He hadn't cried throughout the whole process. All he'd done was scowl and swear. "He's dead—he can't hurt anybody."

"It's okay," Roddy said softly, sitting beside him and touching his thigh lightly. "We got him, and we'll take care of it. You can't stop what other people think, and it don't matter anyway. You got to let it go for your own good."

The advice was sound, but the tone in his voice startled me. Ever since Roddy had come to the house, he'd been helping Kevin with patient care, food prep, serving, and other tasks. They'd rarely been apart. Either I'd overlooked it or missed it because…well, I tended to miss those things, but they were falling in love. I heard it in Roddy's gentle, cautious words and saw it in the rear-view mirror as Kevin reached down and squeezed Roddy's hand. And the way Spence looked at me, he'd seen it too.

I didn't see it ending well.

Spence broke the silence. "You guys think Allen and Levon are well enough to come to the park with us?"

"Bobby said he'd try to get them ready," Kevin said, "but I dunno. They both had a really bad night, and I don't think Allen'll be able to walk very far. He's pretty weak."

"Where do you want to scatter the ashes?" I asked.

"Off a bridge in the Ramble. Doesn't matter which one. The closest, I guess, for Allen."

"Gotcha," Spence said. "West Sixty-Sixth it is. We're almost to the house now."

When we pulled up, we saw Bobby and Theo and Steven sitting on the stoop around Allen, all wearing their winter jackets against the early November breeze. They helped him to his feet as Spence parked in front of the hydrant. Kevin and Roddy climbed into the front seat with us, and the rest of the boys got Allen in the back. True to form, Bobby delivered bad news. He loved doing that. Theo and Steven, of course, argued about it like they did everything. Typical roommates.

"Levon puked up breakfast," Bobby said. "We cleaned him up and put him back to bed, but he's pretty out of it."

"Please tell me you used the Glade," Kevin said. "Nothin' worse than the smell of puke."

"We used, like, half a can," Theo said.

Steven rolled his eyes. "Not that much," he said.

"Yes, it was."

"No. It *wasn't*."

"Boys, *boys*," Spence said, looking at them in the rearview mirror. "Don't *make* me turn this car around."

Everyone chuckled, even Kevin. The weight had been lifted, if only for the time it took us to get to the park. Spence pulled over to the curb amidst honking and a host of middle fingers hoisted out of open car windows. "You guys get out and wait with Allen—I'll be back as soon as I find a space."

We managed to get him to a bench near the entrance, milling around while we waited. Theo and Steven sat on either side of him with Bobby next to Theo. Four men skinny enough to fit on one bench even in their winter coats, Allen pale and absolutely gaunt. They even looked sick, drawing quick glances from passers-by. Kevin seemed fine, if tired, but Roddy had thrived during his time in the house. He was gaining weight and proving to be an invaluable help to Kevin. He was even talking about getting a job and bringing some money into the house to pay us back for his stay.

Spence came back in about ten minutes, having miraculously found a spot only a couple of blocks away. "I know just the place to do this," Roddy said as we entered the park. "It's really pretty and not too far away."

"Don't worry about me," Allen said, breathing hard enough to justify our caution. We took rests whenever we found a vacant bench, so our progress was slow but steady. Even when we were walking, joggers passed us like we were standing still, and we saw the usual complement of cruisers and rent boys gathered in dark, leafy corners—some as thin and sickly looking as our group, waiting for johns with enough money and pent-up libido to play AIDS roulette.

"It's not far now," Roddy said as we were getting up from one of those rests. He stepped back to give the other guys room to get Allen up, and he bumped into a bag lady passing by.

"Watch it, faggot," she snarled.

"Excuse me?"

She stopped and looked at him defiantly, leaning on her rubber-tipped cane. She wore plaid snow pants over stained long johns cinched halfway up her waist, holding down three sweaters of various shades. Her wizened face was ruddy from the cool weather, and she wore a black stocking cap down low over her stringy, iron-grey hair. She smelled of sour sweat with a hint of liniment as she shifted a half-full black garbage bag from one grimy-gloved hand to the other.

"I didn't stutter," she said, jerking her head in the direction of the rent boys. "You queers are takin' over the park. Alla ya got the goddamn AIDS, too."

"Fuck off."

"*You* fuck off." She started to shuffle away, but then she looked back at Kevin. "Whatcha got in the box, boy?"

"My brother's ashes."

Her face softened somewhat. "Aww. You're gonna scatter 'em off the bridge?"

"Thinkin' about it."

Her scowl returned, angrier than before. "*Not in my goddamn park!*"

With uncanny speed and accuracy, she brought her cane up and hit the bottom of the box, knocking it a good two feet in the air. The top popped off and covered us all with a fine coat of remains before it clattered to the ground, spilling out the rest on the sidewalk. Kevin let out an incoherent cry and sank to his knees, trying to scoop up what was left. The rest of us stood there in shock as she clomped quickly away.

"*Crazy fuckin' bitch*!" Roddy said, kneeling down to help Kevin as everyone started shouting at her at once. Allen closed his eyes and sat back down on the bench, breathing heavily. Spence started after her, but I grabbed his arm.

"What are you going to do? Beat up a bag lady?" I said, brushing ash out of my hair. "Besides, we need to help Kevin."

The dam of stoic anger he'd built had cracked, and his sobs began leaking through. His shoulders heaving, he cried and mumbled to himself and Roddy as he tried again and again to pick up ashes and fragments of bone with shaking hands, most of it falling through his fingers back down on the sidewalk, whipped away by the wind. Roddy had a hand on the back of his neck, trying to soothe him and looking up at us.

"Allen don't look too good," he said. "Maybe you guys should get him back home. I'll take care of Kev—we'll catch the subway or somethin.'"

I took a twenty out of my wallet and gave it to him. "Get a cab."

He nodded once, barely acknowledging me before he went back to Kevin—which, I thought, was exactly as it should be. They were good together and, as far as I could see, good for each other. That was going to make their end even harder. For the first time since we'd opened our home to these poor kids, a sense of cold dread gripped me, a finality almost too big for words. I looked back at Roddy with his arms around Kevin, holding him as he sobbed and tried to put his brother's ashes back in the box.

This was going to get much, much worse before it got any better.

Allen held on for a few weeks, but he was gone by Christmas, followed by Levon who had rallied but didn't last more than a few days into 1985. Our empty beds did not stay that way long. Harvey sent us Thomas, Burton, and Armand by Valentine's Day along with Chet and William, who inaugurated the fourth floor. Theo and Bobby died a couple of days apart in early February, but Berkowitz kept supplying patients as his numbers and ours continued to grow.

Roddy was our only success story. He not only flourished, he made good on his promise to get a job. He somehow finagled an assistant cameraman position at WCBS, working there during the day and helping Kevin out with meal prep and serving and evening rounds. He kept enough money to live on but put the rest into Mercedes General. He moved into Kevin's room not long after Levon died, and we sent them to the Ritz-Carlton for a long Valentine's Day weekend, even though Kevin called in no less than seven times checking on us.

Berkowitz came more frequently and stayed longer, never charging a dime. In fact, he brought us the occasional check. His sister never did "come around" about Allen, but he guilted her into making a sizeable donation. Berkowitz's partners even chipped in, which was good for our rapidly dwindling building fund, but more and more, Berkowitz's visits were ending with words of caution.

"Speaking as someone who pays a hefty quarterly premium for malpractice insurance," he said one March afternoon over coffee and Kevin's streusel cake, "you guys are walking a fine line."

"What do you mean?" I said, as Kevin refilled our cups and sat down at the kitchen table with us. Spence was still at work.

"I'm talking about liability among other things. Basically, you guys are running a hospice, though it's not accredited and you don't have a doctor or nurse on staff. That may cause you some problems down the road, *if* that's even a road you want to continue down. I mean, I'll keep dropping by and doing what I can, but I've already been warned by my insurance guy that if something happens here and I get sued, I'm not covered."

"If something happens?" Kevin said. "Like what? Someone dies? They're *coming* here to die, doc. You know that. They haven't got anywhere else to go."

"I know, I know," he replied quickly. "And you all do a terrific job of keeping them comfortable until they're—"

"Wait, wait," I interrupted. "Your *insurance* guy told you? How did *he* find out?"

"People talk, Kent," he said, licking streusel from his fingers. "They gossip. And doctors and nurses gossip more than most—especially about AIDS. It's mysterious because we don't know as much about it as we do cancer or heart disease or other health problems, and that makes it a topic of conversation."

The voices in that conversation were about to grow exponentially.

A few days later, I was upstairs in my office busily trying to pound the second draft of *The Stranger Within* into shape, having helped Kevin feed the guys breakfast and drying dishes. I heard the doorbell, and a few moments later, Kevin hollered up the stairs with more urgency than I'd ever heard in his voice. "Kent! *Kent!!*"

I ran to the top of the stairs and looked downstairs in the vestibule. Kevin stood in the doorway, illuminated by the glare of a Steadicam as he blocked the doorway, waving his arms at a young blond woman pointing a mike at him. In the window over the door, I saw a WNBC news van parked across the street. I recognized the blonde as Diane Moseby, a Channel 4 reporter with a reputation for aggressive interviews.

I hurried down the stairs and as soon as I came into view, she shifted her focus to me, trying to edge farther inside as Kevin brought up his knee and elbowed her out again. "Kent Mortenson?" she said, peering around him. "I'm Di—"

"I *know* who you are. And you'd better get the fuck off my stoop before I call the police. You have no business here."

She ignored me, getting her foot inside the door despite Kevin's best efforts. "What's your relationship with Dr. Harvey Berkowitz? Is this the AIDS clinic you're running with him?"

I swung the heavy wooden door closed, hearing the thumps as it hit her foot and the mike. I hoped I'd broken them both. "Across the street, Mort," she said from the other side. She limped across the street and shot in front of the burned-out building Kevin used to reside in. I couldn't hear what she was saying, but I figured it was probably the sound of the shit hitting the fan.

"I tried to keep her out," Kevin said, "but they got the drop on me. Who the fuck expects TV cameras at the front door?"

I patted his shoulder. "It's okay…well, it's not *okay*, but you did what you could."

"I wonder who ratted us out."

"I'd bet money it was someone from Berkowitz's office. Probably Nurse Ratched. Last time I was in, she looked at me like she was sucking on a lemon. I'd better give Spence a call. He deals with this kind of thing better than I do."

"He does? You have TV cameras on your doorstep a lot?"

"Not a *lot*. The last time was about ten years ago when we went to our high school senior prom together. I hated it then, and I think I'm going to hate it even more now. Do we have groceries in the house?"

"Some."

I pulled out my wallet and gave him all the cash I had. "You'd better get what we need for a week. When this hits the news and the locusts descend, you're not going to be able to get out for a while."

"But—"

"Trust me. Get a cab and have him come around to the back door. I'll watch the guys while you're gone."

"You're the boss," he said. Then he grinned. "You guys really went to prom together? Man, that took some balls."

"We were kids. We had no idea what we were letting ourselves in for, and this is going to be ten times worse because it's gay men helping other gay men. Straight people *hate* that. Oh, and you better give Roddy a call and let him know it might be a clusterfuck around here for a few days."

"Maybe I'll see if he can take a couple of days off work. Are we gonna tell the guys?"

"We pretty much have to. They're going to notice the crowd outside."

"You think it'll be that bad?"

"Two gay guys living with a houseful of AIDS patients and one almost underage housekeeper? Yeah. It's going to get bad. I'm calling Spence, then I'm calling our lawyer."

Bless his eighteen-year-old heart, Kevin tried to approach the situation with some positivity, going for a party atmosphere after dinner with a three-layer chocolate cake we ate in front of the TV. Most of the guys either couldn't or didn't want to come down, but Armand and Burt were there along with Kevin and Roddy and Spence and myself.

"We're gonna be famous!" Kevin said to Roddy.

"Notorious is closer to the mark," Spence said, licking frosting off his upper lip. "And you should be careful what you wish for."

We'd both tried to call Berkowitz, but he'd gone to ground and was unreachable. Our lawyer—well, Miss Lee's lawyer—had referred us to a local colleague of his, one Bob Rashkin, who called WNBC immediately to see if he could quash the story. No such luck. Moseby was going ahead with it, which left us eating chocolate cake and waiting through stories about Gorbachev's installation as the head of the Soviet Union, the

Iraqi raid on Tehran, and Harrod's being sold to Mohamed Al-Fayed until blow-dried talking head Chuck Scarborough finally appeared on screen.

"Knicks over the Hawks by four, mild in the five boroughs until the rain moves in at midnight, and an AIDS death house on the Upper West Side. All these local stories and more after the break here on Channel 4 news."

"AIDS death house," I repeated. "So that's how they're going to play it."

"It doesn't exactly roll off the tongue," Spence said. "You'd think they could have come up with something catchier."

"It's all that journalistic integrity."

Armand clucked his tongue. "I can't believe you guys aren't taking this seriously. I mean, my mom's going to be watching this."

"If your mom gave a shit, you wouldn't be here," Kevin said, looking back at him.

Roddy put his hand on Kevin's arm. "*Cállate, mi amor.*"

Spence also looked Armand's way. "We *are* taking it seriously, but this kind of thing takes a sense of humor to survive, trust me. The lawyer already sent a statement to Moseby. I just hope she reads it on air."

As the last commercial jingle faded away, they went to a two-shot of the anchor and Diane Moseby. She looked blonder and more tanned than she did in person, her hair styled in a tidy, shoulder-length flip that bounced perkily when she moved her head.

"So, what's going on in the Upper West Side, Diane?"

The camera dollied in for her one-shot, a graphics box

opening up to the right with a blurred image of what looked like Dr. Berkowitz.

"Plenty, Chuck," she said. *"Five young men have died in the care of what can only be called an informal AIDS hospice. These and other patients were referred to a brownstone on W. 80th by Dr. Harvey Berkowitz of the Tannhauser Clinic, where they spent their last days with the owners of the brownstone, two homosexual men, Kent Mortenson and Spencer Michalek, along with their seventeen-year-old housekeeper..."* She raised one eyebrow. *"...Kevin Borden, a brother to one of the deceased."*

"Did you introduce yourself?" I said to Kevin.

"Not hardly."

"She must have gotten that from Nurse Ratched," Spence said.

"We attempted to speak with Dr. Berkowitz—could you please roll that, guys?"

The graphics box came alive, Berkowitz in motion blocking the mikes and waving his right hand as he pulled his hat down with the left. "Dr. Berkowitz," she said, "could you tell us what happened to Riley Borden? Or your nephew Allen Hauschmidt? Or Levon Sarchet? How about Theodore Pullman and Robert Schuler?" With every name, he stepped a bit quicker and pulled his hat down further as he crossed the parking lot.

"No comment," he finally said as he got into his car and slammed the door.

"We received a similar welcome at the brownstone where the deaths took place."

Our front door then appeared in the graphics box, first me yelling with Kevin looking over my shoulder, then the slam and stumble from Moseby.

"*Mortenson and Michalek were also involved in an incident a decade ago when they attended their senior high school prom together, drawing a protest from The Founder's Focus Group that resulted in the death of an infant.*"

"A baby?" Kevin asked. "Is that true?"

"Unfortunately," I replied.

"*We were not able to speak with anyone at the brownstone, but we have been provided with a statement through their attorney, Robert Haskins: 'Although Mr. Mortenson, Mr. Michalek, and Mr. Borden are not licensed doctors or nurses, the care they have provided these and other young men during their final days is comparable to what a family might give had they not been turned away due to the stigma of their disease. These men were dying and homeless and had nowhere else to turn, and my clients should be applauded for their efforts, not vilified.'*"

"And she even read the whole thing," Spence said.

"*One person not clapping is local community board president Kristie Boniface, who questions the legitimacy of the enterprise in terms of zoning.*" The graphics box showed an angular-looking brunette with heavy, red lipstick and too much blush. She stood outside, the breeze blowing her hair back from her face.

"*This is a strictly residential area*" she said, "*and if they don't have a variance, they're going to have to shut down. We intend on pursuing this aggressively with the city.*" The box disappeared.

"Big surprise," Roddy said. "We don't have one of those variance things, do we?"

Spence put his plate on the coffee table. "Haskins is working on it. He's going to come by tomorrow."

"According to the city's records, no such variance has either been applied for or granted. The next city council meeting is next Tuesday, so we'll be watching closely and I'll be there with a special report. Back to you, Chuck."

I grabbed the remote and clicked the TV off. The dot in the middle of the screen hadn't even faded before the phone rang. Kevin and Roddy collected the plates and Armand went back upstairs as I answered it, Spence standing nearby.

"Hello?"

"Kent? It's Berkowitz. Did you see the news?"

Spence leaned in to hear better. "Oh, we saw it all right," I said. "Nice ducking."

"You weren't so bad on the stoop, either. Listen, I'm calling because—"

"Let me guess. The clinic either fired you or is about to fire you, your insurance cancelled you, and you're not going to come around anymore, leaving us high and dry. That about the size of it?" I could hear my voice rising and feel Spence's arm on my shoulder. He bent close to the receiver.

Berkowitz was quiet for a beat. "No," he said calmly, "not quite. My premium's paid, so they can't cancel me for at least three months. The clinic *did* call me in to dismiss me, but I told 'em they could fuck the hell off. I quit. Say hello to your new staff doctor, smart ass."

Spence's mouth was open as far as mine was. "You're kidding," I said.

"I'm not. Asa and I have been talking it over ever since Allen died. What you guys did for him was amazing. I'm not sure we'll ever be able to thank you enough. The least we can do is stand

140

by you and make sure these guys get the care they need. And if that means giving up the place on Fire Island or whatever, so be it. This is more important. We're working on a statement for the press right now, and you and Spence should be doing the same thing even though your lawyer prepared something— could you give me his number, by the way? I've already had calls from AP and UPI, so it won't be long before this hits the wires. And then the shit's really gonna hit the fan."

"We know," I said, still somewhat stunned. "We've been through this before."

"So I gather. I want to hear about that, but not right now. Lots to do. I'll come by tomorrow. Back way, of course. Talk to you then."

He hung up and left us staring at the phone.

The crowds didn't start to gather until the next morning. There seemed to be more foot traffic than usual for our neighborhood the rest of the night, but the dawn brought a small knot of people clutching thermoses of coffee. The sidewalk was still pretty clear by ten o'clock when both Haskins and Berkowitz showed up for a strategy meeting.

By request of his rather conservative architectural firm, Spence was staying home for a few days. "I think they're gonna fire me," he said as he and Haskins and Berkowitz gathered around the kitchen table. Haskins started giving Spence advice, and that's when I left the room. Kevin was cleaning up from breakfast and doing lunch prep, but I wasn't about to let the fracas keep me from my second draft.

I got a couple of hours in before Kevin called me to help serve lunch, but it was difficult to keep working and not pace by the front window now and then, sizing up the small but peaceful crowd. Spence and Haskins and Berkowitz were on the phone pretty much all morning. Kevin and I finished up lunch while Berkowitz quickly checked in on the guys and began ordering supplies.

About one thirty in the afternoon, Burt came downstairs. "I think Thomas is dead," he said. "He's not breathing."

"Shit," Berkowitz said, taking the stairs two at a time. We all followed him, but it was obvious on entering the room that the poor guy was gone. He'd come in under his own power, but he'd taken to his bed a couple weeks later and never left. I don't think I ever saw him eat solid food. He was one of two guys on IV fluids, but Chet at least had moments of lucidity and seemed to be getting better. Thomas never woke up.

"Do we know where his family is?" Kevin asked.

"It's on his clinic intake form," Berkowitz said. "I'll sign the death certificate and make some calls, but you know what's going to happen when the mortuary shows up."

"All too well."

We were the lead story on the six o'clock news.

SIXTH FATALITY AT AIDS DEATH HOUSE ON UWS
UWS AIDS DEATH HOUSE CLAIMS SIXTH VICTIM
SIX MEN DEAD AT UWS AIDS DEATH HOUSE

"I'm sensing a pattern here," Spence said, tossing the morning papers on the kitchen table as Kevin poured coffee and sat down with us. "Where's Roddy?"

"Sleepin' in," Kevin said, picking up one of the papers. "Damn, these fuckers are brutal. I mean, 'AIDS death house'? Really?"

I shrugged. "It sells papers."

"But it's wrong."

"If it sells papers, it doesn't matter. What's for breakfast?"

"Yesterday's coffee cake. I gotta get the oatmeal goin' for the guys." He stood up, took a foil-wrapped plate out of the bread-box, and put it on the table. "I'm surprised Berkowitz left any. Man, that dude can eat. Want me to plug the phone back in?"

"Not just yet," I said. "I'm enjoying the quiet."

"It did get kinda crazy here yesterday," he said, getting a stock pot from the cupboard beneath the sink. As he filled it with water, he parted the curtains over the sink and peered across the street. "Jesus, the news vans are over there already. It's not even six."

"Are the protesters out yet?" Spence asked.

"A few. I think that community board lady's one of 'em."

"No doubt," I said. "That's an elected position, so she's going to be wherever the news vans are."

Spence dunked a corner of the pastry in his coffee. "Cynic."

"That's me. Did you hear from work?"

He shook his head. "Doesn't matter. I think I can steal enough clients to go freelance."

"Won't that piss them off?"

"What are they gonna do, fire me?" He finished the piece of coffee cake in two bites. "Get anything done on the book yesterday?"

"Not much. Too many distractions. Today's probably going to be worse."

"Much worse," Kevin said. He motioned us over and let the curtain fall as he carried the stockpot to the stove. "Check it out."

We put our heads side by side at the narrow window, watching in horror as two vans parked and began to disgorge a phalanx of middle-aged matrons wearing pillbox hats and carrying placards. A brunette with a bullhorn went over to greet them, issuing placement instructions through said amplification device shortly thereafter.

"Holy Jesus," Spence said. "There must be fifty or sixty people out there."

"At least," I said.

Spence snorted. "Well, she might be hot shit with the zoning board, but she seems to have forgotten the noise ordinance. They can't fire up all that hatred before eight, so I'm plugging the phone in and calling the cops right now."

"You know the noise ordinance?" I asked.

"Haskins told us yesterday—eight a.m. to ten p.m. And I'm gonna make damn sure they stick to it." He strode angrily to the phone nook and bent over the plug, leaving me looking out the window. As the vans pulled away, a cab stopped in front of the house, but it was too near the building to see who got out.

"What's goin' on?" Roddy asked as he padded barefoot out of his and Kevin's room into the kitchen, wearing his ratty brown bathrobe. He kissed Kevin on the cheek as Kevin dumped oatmeal into the stockpot.

"Mayhem," Kevin said over the ringing of the doorbell.

144

"Somebody get that—I'm on the phone."

Roddy went for the coffeepot as I slid out of the kitchen and looked through the peephole. Whoever it was had their head turned toward the fracas across the street. I clucked my tongue and threw open the door, ready to chop somebody down to size.

"So," Miss Lee said, "I have to watch the evening news to find out what you're doing with my money? Let me in before those old biddies think I'm with them."

Despite my surprise at seeing her, I had to chuckle as I stepped aside. In her mid-seventies, she was well into old biddy territory herself, though she'd never admit it. And she wouldn't be caught dead across the street. She breezed past me and put down the old black Samsonite suitcase I remembered from the top shelf of the hall closet in the big house, dropping her coat on top of it. Then she stretched her arms wide.

"What are you doing here?" I asked, hugging her tightly and smelling her lilac sachet.

"Rendering aid and comfort to the enemy," she said. "Where's my other boy?" She craned her neck and looked past me, waving to Spence in the phone nook. He looked as surprised as I did, faltering just a touch in his tirade to the police before holding up a finger and continuing.

"Did you just get in?"

She stared past me again, looking at Kevin and Roddy in the doorway to the kitchen. "About an hour ago," she said. "Bob Haskins called me last night. After I saw the news, I got a bee in my bonnet, packed, and took—what do they call it—a redeye to La Guardia, and here I am. Lord, that was a long taxi ride. Who are these fine-looking young gentlemen?"

"Kevin Borden, ma'am," Kevin said, stepping forward as he wiped his hands with a dishtowel, "and this is my boyfriend, Rodolfo Fuentes." Roddy just stared and re-tied his bathrobe. Kevin elbowed him. "Jeez, put some clothes on." Roddy sidled past us while Kevin stuck his now-dry hand out. "You must be Miss Lee."

"I must be," she said, ignoring his hand and going in for a quick hug. "Mr. Haskins says you run a pretty tight ship taking care of the house and all. How old are you?"

"Eighteen, ma'am."

"Call me Miss Lee. Ma'am's for those old fussbudgets out there. Sorry to hear you lost your brother—Riley, was it?"

"Yes'm…Miss Lee. Thank you."

Spence appeared behind her carrying her suitcase as he gave her a one-armed hug. "It's great to see you, Miss Lee. I'll put this in our room. We'll take the fold out sofa."

"You'll do no such thing," she said, putting an arm around his waist. "I came here to help, not put you out. I'll take the sofa, and that's all there is to that. You boys are doing the right thing no matter what anyone else says. Taking care of your own. That's what you're *supposed* to do."

I could have sworn I saw a tear in Kevin's eye. "I gotta check the oatmeal," he said. "S'cuse me."

"You got a cup of coffee for an old lady?" she said, following him.

"I'll make fresh."

Two hours later, Kevin and Miss Lee had fed breakfast to William, Armand, Burt, Chet, and Harrison and Daniel, our two newest arrivals on the fourth floor, picked up the day before Diane Moseby entered our lives. Kevin had shown her who needed to be fed by hand, who could eat by himself, and how to change Burt's IV bag. Roddy and Spence had been sent out for last minute supplies, and I had been confined to my office. "You have a book to write, young man," Miss Lee reminded me.

We kept the phone plugged in and the answering machine on but turned the ringer and the sound off. At eight on the dot, the general hubbub started, though they thankfully eschewed the use of the bullhorn for the time being. The signs were the usual level of hurtful: DEATH TO THE DEATH HOUSE, AIDS KILLS FAGS DEAD, NOT IN *MY* NEIGHBORHOOD, and HONK IF YOU HATE FAGGOTS. Despite the noise and occasional volley of honks, Miss Lee opted for a nap since she hadn't slept much on the plane.

"Don't worry about me," she said. "I brought earplugs. I figured they'd come in handy in the city. Just get me up when you're ready to put lunch out."

I tried to get some writing done, but Armand was restless across the hall. I could hear his floorboards creaking as he paced, and I figured he was probably missing Thomas—not that Thomas had ever been conscious. As he did at least once every day for some reason, he stuck his head in my office. "Has my mom called today?" Always the same question.

"I don't think so, Armand—you want me to check the messages?"

He seemed to consider this for a moment. "No, it's okay," he said. "I'd know." And then he went back to his room.

I had no idea *how* he'd know, but I also had no doubt he would. Armand always seemed otherworldly to me. He was tall and almost skeletally thin due to his illness, his hair shorn close enough to see the lesions on his scalp. His deep blue, almost violet, eyes masked what felt like a preternatural intuition of unknown origin. He floated around the house with stealthy grace, his lanky arrival never heralded by the sound of footsteps. He'd simply appear, inquisitive yet all-knowing, usually asking a question.

He looked in my doorway once again. "Could you get them to stop making noise?"

"Who?"

"The people outside."

"I wish I could," I said. "If you want, Miss Lee probably has some spare earplugs so they didn't bother you as much if you wanted to read or something."

He scrunched up his nose. "I'd still feel them out there. Thanks, anyway." And he was gone again.

I was actually able to work on the book for an hour or so before I heard Spence and Roddy downstairs. Spence jumped on the phone and, from what I could hear, was talking to potential clients. I also heard Kevin and Roddy working on sloppy joes and chips for lunch, chided mildly by Miss Lee for letting her sleep instead of getting her up as instructed. It's amazing how much you can hear when you're trying to avoid writing. What I suddenly did *not* hear was the crowd outside.

When I looked out the window, to my surprise I saw Armand in his slippers and bathrobe out in the thirty-degree sunshine crossing the street, calmly waiting for traffic to clear as he headed directly for the group of protesters. As he approached, they had fallen nearly silent, just watching him. I was torn. Every instinct I had told me to go out and get him, but did I really want to do that? He may have been in our care, but he was hardly a prisoner. Who were we to keep him from expressing any sentiment he may have directly to them?

As no one else came rushing out to collect him, either they felt the same way or hadn't noticed he was gone. I raced downstairs so I didn't miss anything. "Hey," I said as I hit the first floor and slid into the kitchen, "Armand's—"

"We know," Spence said. He and Miss Lee and Kevin and Roddy were all crowded around the kitchen window.

"He didn't say a word to anybody," Roddy said. "He just came down and went out the damn door."

Miss Lee clucked her tongue. "That poor boy—he'll catch his death without a jacket."

"He sure shut 'em up," Kevin said, going back to the stove to stir the sloppy joe mixture.

When Armand hit the other side of the street, he made a beeline for the one van left. Its door was open, and you could see from the signs leaning up against it that was where the placards were stored. People began shouting at him, but no one touched him. In fact, they shrank back in fear even as they yelled. This was probably the closest many of them had been to a man with AIDS, and they weren't quite sure how to deal with it. He had the element of surprise and was taking advantage of it brilliantly, turning his back on them as he rummaged inside their van.

"I think he's making his own sign," Spence said.

"Now *that's* balls," Roddy said. "Sorry, Miss Lee."

The crowd got louder but no closer as he turned around and displayed his surprisingly firm and solid block printing: PLEASE LET US DIE IN PEACE.

Some people shouted, some people snorted, but most turned to each other in stunned reassurance that this was really happening. Armand held the placard in front of him as if it were a crucifix, warding off the bystanders as he calmly walked back across the street and sat down on our stoop, holding the sign up for all to see.

The reporters adjusted their vantage points, getting various shots of Armand and his sign. Now that he was safely across the street once again, the jeers and catcalls started in earnest, louder than before. Some even threw rocks. None came very close, but one of the honking cars circled the block and got him with a Styrofoam cup of coffee hurled out the driver's side window. Armand wiped his face and the sign with the hem of his robe but remained sitting there.

Miss Lee grabbed my shoulder. "We have to get him inside," she said.

I opened the door, creating a fresh brouhaha from the crowd. "Armand? Why don't you come inside? We can hang that out the window if you want."

"Why?" he said, looking genuinely perplexed. "*They're* outside."

I couldn't argue with that, but I had an inspiration. "Your mother's on the phone."

He looked at me with the barest hint of a grin, his hair still wet from the coffee. "No, she isn't."

Miss Lee knelt down beside him. "We're afraid you'll get hurt," she said. "Please come inside."

He shook his head. "I'd prefer not to," he replied, a beatific Bartleby.

I could feel the frustration coming off Miss Lee in waves. She stood up and made herself heard *sans* bullhorn. "*YOU PEOPLE ARE VILE!! WHERE'S YOUR HUMANITY? THIS COULD BE YOUR SON!!*"

Of the two of them, I thought it best to get Miss Lee back inside before she could aggravate the situation. I was just glad she didn't have her rifle. I shooed her in and shut the door. "I'll watch him. I don't know what else I can do—why don't you help Kevin with lunch? Maybe he'll come in after a while."

But he didn't. He stayed out there, silent and immoveable all through lunch and dinner both. Only when the protesters called it a day and piled in the van did we hear him come in and close the door behind him. Kevin and Miss Lee were washing dishes and I was drying. He moved slowly, sitting down at the table. "Maybe I could get a sandwich?" he asked.

"Sure," Kevin said. "Ham? Salami?"

"Ham, please. No mustard."

"Comin' right up."

For the first time since I'd known her, Miss Lee seemed lost for words. She kept giving him curious glances, but she stopped just shy of asking him about the whole episode. I kept drying dishes, and Kevin made Armand's sandwich. "You can take it up to your room if you want," he said, putting the plate in front of him.

"I'll just eat it here if that's okay. I'm so tired all of a sudden." Then he leaned back in the chair, his head slumping to his chest.

"Oh my God," Miss Lee said. "Armand? Are you okay?"

He didn't answer.

Kevin took Armand's hand and checked his pulse, then he shook his head. "Get Berkowitz. He's gone."

Miss Lee gave a small sob, hugged him, then sat down and cried.

His mother never did call.

"It's not a *regular* disease—you know, something you get like heart disease or cancer," said the heavyset brunette with the tall, lacquered bouffant. Her makeup was caked thick, creasing the corners of her mean mouth. "You have to be a *deviant*," she said, looking at us. "And we don't want that sort of thing in our neighborhood." She sat down amidst applause from the near standing room only crowd.

All seven community planning board members looked put out and weary of hearing the same thing. We must have been in that cramped, crabbed room for a couple of hours listening to people complain about us. About the nicest thing anyone had to say was that our establishment wasn't in line with the sort of tax revenue they'd expected to generate in that neighborhood. Never mind the fact that the only neighbor in our immediate vicinity were an overpriced Chinese restaurant, a deli with kosher cockroaches, and a shitload of burned-out buildings. Our zoning variance application looked dead in the water.

Both Spence and Miss Lee were drowsing, and even Bob Haskins looked tired of the proceedings. Kevin and Roddy had stayed back at the house to take care of the guys we had left. No one had died since Armand a couple of weeks back, but almost all of them had gotten worse. We couldn't directly trace their decline to the constant noise and negative atmosphere, but we were sure it hadn't helped.

The only person who looked alert was Dr. Berkowitz, who kept looking back at the entrance as if he was expecting something to happen. As he checked his watch for the umpteenth time, the door opened and in walked a sleek, stylish middle-aged woman dressed in a dark purple blouse and a knee-length black skirt. She patted her perfectly coiffed hair and glanced around the room. Berkowitz smiled and waved her over, but she remained in front of the door.

"Okay," the head of the board said, picking up his gavel, "if that's all the public comment, I think we can put this to a vo—"

"Just a minute," the woman said in a clear, loud voice. "I have something to say."

Everyone awake now, they turned their heads to the back of the room as he sighed and put his gavel back down. "Go ahead," he said with a wave of his hand. "Keep it to five minutes, ma'am."

She nodded curtly and looked around. "My name is Sheila Hauschmidt. My son, Allen, died while in the care of these gentlemen, and I thank God for them every day of my life. I could not have done what they did for him. You see, he never told us he was…that way. We only found out when it was too late. I was too angry and hurt to be as compassionate or caring as I should have. I would have been resentful if he'd put me in that position—too resentful to make his last days anything other than difficult. I couldn't even speak to him. How could I have cared for him?"

She paused a second, her eyes hard and dry. "These men provided a home for him at the end, one where he could die with the dignity and respect I wasn't able to force. I don't know how I can reconcile or even live with his death for the rest of my life, but as small a comfort as it is, I know he wasn't alone thanks to them."

The brunette stood up. "Very touching, dearie. Where did you say you lived?"

"I didn't, but I live in Scarsdale."

"Well, maybe you should let them open one up there."

Mrs. Hauschmidt left without another word. Berkowitz got up and followed her out the door, leaving us to face the vote alone, but we all knew how it would go.

Seven members, seven "no" votes. Unanimous rejection.

"Variance denied," the man with the gavel said. "Meeting adjourned."

"That figures," Kevin said, putting the chocolate cake out on the kitchen table and doling out the dessert plates. "Fuckers—sorry, Miss Lee."

"You won't get an argument out of me," she said, looking suspiciously at the dessert. "This isn't from a box, is it?"

"No way. It's the yellow cake recipe you wrote down. Frosting, too."

She started slicing and serving. "Looks delicious," she said. "Good texture—frosting might be a bit grainy, but you'll get it." She lit up when she took a bite. "Absolutely delicious. High marks from me, mister."

"And me," Berkowitz said. "I wish Asa could bake this well."

Kevin smiled and blushed from the neck up.

"So, what happens now?" Roddy asked.

Haskins sipped his coffee. "Technically, nothing. The cops aren't going to show up at your door in ten days to make sure no one else is living here but you. You could probably still keep on what you're doing for a while, but we've come up with another solution."

"Plan B," Miss Lee said.

"Plan B?" Spence said. "I didn't know we *had* a plan B."

"Spencer Michalek, how long have you known me? I *always* have a plan B. And it involves the house you and your mother used to live in."

"How so?"

She waved her fork in the air. "Developers have been after that land for years, maybe a quarter of the way up the mountain. Luxury homes, don't you know."

"You'd sell that off?" I asked.

She shrugged. "I'd still have three-quarters of a mountain to myself. Can't see it'd make that much difference. They're offering me more money than I'd ever be able to spend. I'd be able to fund something along the lines of what you're doing here only with regular doctors and nurses. Dr. Berkowitz here thinks—well, why don't *you* tell them what you think?"

"This is only the tip of the AIDS iceberg," he said. "It's going to eventually spread to the straight population, starting with IV drug users, but it's going to decimate us. Gay men think they're invincible, but they're wrong. A lot of people are going to die before they start paying attention. Or before we even *hope* to get government funding."

Haskins finished his cake and sat back in his chair—the very one Armand had died in. "We found a sweet little property close to Mount Sinai, a fifty-bed facility with room to grow, but it needs some work. We were hoping Spence might be able to do a quick redesign of the interior if he's not too busy with his other clients. For his usual fee, of course."

"I'll get to work on it right away."

"And we were hoping you two would be on the board of directors. There's even a place for Kevin to run the kitchen if he's so inclined."

"Me? Oh man, I can't do that. I'm not a nutritionist."

Miss Lee laughed. "You will be by the time you're out of cooking school," she said. "Trust fund's already set up—if Kent doesn't mind managing it."

"My pleasure. Just tell me what I have to do."

"Bob'll tell you. He's the lawyer."

"You got to be kiddin' me—I'm going to cooking school? Oh. My. God." He and Roddy grinned widely at each other. "This is unbelievable. Thank you, Miss Lee. You...you..." He couldn't finish his sentence before the tears started falling. He stood up and hugged her.

"Dammit, that means we have to find another Hazel," I said.

"No way," he said, looking up from his hug. "We'll make it work. Maybe Roddy and I can take one of the big rooms on the third floor?"

"Whatever makes you happy," Spence said.

1:27 a.m., and I was wide awake, which wasn't uncommon. I've always been a light sleeper, and having the guys in the house didn't help that. Sometimes I'd get up in the middle of the night and check on them, but not tonight. I eased out of bed so as not to wake Spence, then went to the window.

The moon was full and shone down on the thankfully empty space across the street. No protesters or vans, just a cracked sidewalk without even a random drunk in sight. It was even fairly quiet despite the ambient noise New Yorkers have long since learned to tune out. Suddenly, I saw a pair of headlights cut through the dark, a taxi stopping in front of our house. The hairs on the back of my neck started to rise in fear, but then I heard our door open and close ever so softly.

Miss Lee hefted her black Samsonite into the rear seat and then joined it. After a few moments, they took off. I smiled. Typical Miss Lee, I thought. She came, she saw, she conquered, and then she left again. I put my slippers on and went downstairs as quietly as I could, but I doubted anyone could hear me over Kevin's snoring. He slept as hard as he worked. I heard a piece of cake calling my name, so I cut a slice and poured a glass of milk, taking them over to the table where I saw Miss Lee's folded over note.

Boys—

Sorry for leaving in the middle of the night, but you know how I hate saying goodbye. I can only take the city for so long before I start missing my mountain, my front porch, my flannel shirts, and my rocking chair. Thank you for your generous hospitality and allowing me to be a part of Mercedes General. I can't tell you how proud I am of all of you and what you're doing. You are the finest people I know, and I mean that with all my heart. Take care, and I'll call you when I get back home.

Miss Lee

I smiled, refolded it, and put it back where I found it. I finished my cake and milk, then went into the living room, which was still redolent of her lilac sachet. The house already felt empty and would seem emptier once the guys were moved to the new facility, but for now I let myself be ten years old again, full of cake and milk and Miss Lee's scent.

I had the rest of my life to be an adult.

ANOTHER DEATH, ANOTHER PATH

April 19, 2006

was already up late reading, but Spence sat up in bed just before the phone rang. "She's gone," he said.

"What? Who?" I knocked my empty waterglass off the night table as I answered the landline. "Hello?"

"Hey Uncle Kent," Chris said. "Look, I'm sorry to be calling you guys this late, but I've got some bad news."

"Miss Lee, right? What happened?" I got up and put on my robe.

I heard his shaky sigh. "Yeah. She's...I just called the ambulance and the doctor, but there's no pulse. She looks pretty peaceful, though, just sitting here. Last night we did a Bette Davis double feature, and she seemed fine. I went home and got a couple hours sleep, but when I got up to pee, I saw the TV room light was on. I had a bad feeling, so I went over and let myself in. She was still in her rocker with a Johnnie Walker nightcap on the coffee table."

"She always did like her Johnnie Walker," I said.

"And she made it to one hundred, just like she always said she would."

"She lived life on her own terms and left it the same way. She was one of a kind."

"I'm gonna miss her so..." He choked back a sob. "Look, I think the doc's here—you want me to pick you up at the airport?"

"Oh God, no. That's an eight-hour round trip for you. We'll get a car. I'll call once we get a flight out."

"United has a two forty-five out of LaGuardia," Spence said, sitting naked in front of the computer. "That'll get us there after seven, so we could be in Coyote by about noon."

"Book it—Chris, Spence says we can be there about noon."

"Cool. See you then."

Spence finished booking the flight and shut the computer down while I got our suitcases down from the top closet shelf.

"Are you okay?" he asked, pulling on a pair of jeans and a sweater. I put both suitcases on the bed and opened them, getting socks and underwear from our dresser and putting them in first. I had a system.

"Yeah. I was sort of expecting it. Weren't you? I'm just glad we were all able to get out there in February for her birthday. Speaking of which, you'd better call Kevin and Roddy in case Chris forgot. He's got a lot to deal with." Jeans and khakis next. Then button-downs I laid out and rolled up.

"Right," he said, putting socks and running shoes on. "What time is it in St. Louis?"

"Late, just like it is here, but they'll want to know." Sweaters on top.

"True." He picked up his phone and went downstairs. By the time I finished packing us and getting dressed, he brought me up a cup of coffee. "They'll be there sometime tomorrow. I called a cab, but I think you have time to slam this down."

"Thanks." I noticed his red eyes. "Are you all right?"

"Yeah. Had kind of a meltdown while I was talking to them, though."

I put my coffee down on the dresser and held out my arms. "C'mere."

Folding him in my arms, I felt him letting go and sobbing on my shoulder. I patted his back gently, trying to soothe him. But I actually felt a bit jealous. He'd always been able to express sadness like this, whereas I'm much more detached, especially after Mercedes General. Those boys sucked me dry of grief and left me with nothing to replace it except emptiness. It doesn't mean I don't feel things as keenly as others, but I just don't show it. I always wondered if that would change when someone as important to me as Miss Lee died, but it hadn't so far.

Spence had finished for the time being, but he was far from being done. He wiped his eyes as he looked at me. "Sorry," he said.

"Don't apologize. You feel what you feel." I retrieved my coffee and drank it in two gulps. "We should get downstairs and wait for the taxi—I packed blue and black for you. Do you want anything special?"

"I don't think so. The last I remember, she just wanted a simple ash-scattering, so there won't be any big funeral or ceremony or anything unless Chris sets something up. And he hates people as much as she did, so I can't see that happening."

Out of the corner of my eye, I saw headlights outside. "I think the cab's here. You ready to do this?"

"As ready as I'm ever going to get. Let's go."

I have no empirical evidence to prove it, but the gates for flights leaving in the middle of the night seem to be stocked with the most desperate airline passengers. The ones who aren't sleeping are ridden with anxiety, all shifting limbs and restless eyes. They're either running from or going to an emergency, and the fortyish, red-haired woman sitting across from Spence looked like no exception.

Her cheeks were wet, and her eyes were red and smeary. She was wearing dark blue sweatpants and an oversized grey hoodie. Her short-laced Nikes were untied, and she sat with one leg tucked beneath her, looking around as she clutched a balled-up handkerchief in one tight fist.

"Bet you're glad you got that manuscript off to Sidney yesterday," he said to me as she snapped her head toward us.

I sighed. Sometimes I wished he'd look around before he speaks. "Yeah," I said, trying to brush it off as well as I could.

"Excuse me," she said. "I couldn't help overhearing—are you a writer?"

Trapped, I tried smiling, but I'm afraid it looked more like a grimace. "Yes."

"I read a lot. Would I know you?"

"Maybe," I said. "Kent Mortenson?"

Her red-rimmed eyes lit up, and she unzipped the backpack

on the seat next to her, grinning as she reached inside and took out a copy of 'Nathan's Time.' "The 'Nathan Burgoine detective series, right? God, I *love* those. How did you ever come up with a gay detective who sings opera?" She went back in the backpack for a pen and held both out for me. "Would you, please? My name's Evelyn."

"Of course," I said. Sometimes I hated the series and sometimes I loved it, but after an even dozen books, I was pretty much done with the whole affair. *The New York Times* bestseller list crossover was great and the money had been terrific, but I wish someone would remember the three books I'd written before 'Nathan's Aria, the first one in the series The 'Nathan I was signing was number four. Or five. I'd lost track. All I knew for certain was the manuscript I'd just sent my agent was the last—'Nathan's Exit. After twelve years, I'd finally killed him off. "Evelyn, you said?"

"E-V-E-L-Y-N," she replied. "I can't believe I ran into you." She looked at Spence. "And you must be his partner. I'll bet you're proud of him."

"Correct on both counts," Spence said with a smile.

I signed the book and handed it back to her. "There you are. Thanks for being a loyal reader."

She glanced at the inscription and put the book back in her backpack. "Thanks for signing it. So, where are you guys off to so early? Book business?"

I was about to nod in an attempt to bring the encounter to a close, but Spence's grief was too great to keep bottled in. "Death in the family," he said gravely.

The hint of the smile she had for the signed book disappeared, and she instantly looked as morose as she had before she started talking to us. "Oh no," she said. "Me too. Was it someone you were close to?" She mostly kept her eyes on Spence but glanced at me.

I know it was mean, but my first thought was that we wouldn't be traveling at this time of the morning for a casual acquaintance.

"Our grandmother—well, Kent's grandmother. But she practically raised us."

"Oh, I'm so sorry. It's the same thing with my aunt. She took me in when I was a little girl. My mom died and…"

Her face screwed up and she burst into tears, blotting her eyes with the wad of handkerchief as she untucked her leg, put her foot on the floor, and leaned forward a bit. Spence, who couldn't watch someone cry without joining in, reached awkwardly across the narrow aisle and hugged her as best he could.

"It's okay," he choked out. "It'll be okay." And then, as I knew he would, he started crying himself. If they had been standing, they would have fallen into each other's arms in luxurious grief, but the best they could manage was a tenuous embrace. Its tentativeness, however, did not affect its fervency. They both sobbed openly, attracting the attention of the passengers as well as the flight crew preparing to board.

I couldn't do much but watch along with everyone else. It was a bit odd looking, I'm sure, but it was well within reason considering Spence's reaction to grief as well as my own. He needed to share it with someone, and I didn't. I just wasn't built that way, and I'd long ago stopped caring what anyone else thought of us. Let them cry their hearts out to each other. He'd sleep well all the way to Denver and so, I was certain, would she.

After what seemed like an eternity, they finally fell silent and spent, disentangling from each other as Spence fell into his seat and she into hers. Spence looked sated. She looked embarrassed. He put his hand between the seats and grasped mine tightly. I gripped back and smiled, letting him know I understood. I wasn't sure he needed that confirmation, but I gave it to him anyway.

"I'm sorry," Evelyn said, though it was hard to tell whether she was speaking to me or Spence. "That was *so* inappropriate."

As I couldn't tell if she was talking to me, I decided not to engage. I'd signed her book and done my job, and I was happy to leave further interaction up to Spence. They had more in common anyway. At times like this, I wished I could read in airports but something about them forbids my processing anyone else's words. If I get bored watching people, I have to go into my head and work on plots or dialogue instead.

"Don't worry about it," Spence said to her. "I guess I needed it as much as you did."

The gate attendant picked up her handheld mic and announced boarding for first class.

"That's us," I said, standing up and shouldering my coat and laptop bag as Spence did the same. "Very nice meeting you, Evelyn," I said, relieved she hadn't also stood up. "Condolences on your aunt, and thank you for reading."

She smiled again. "Thanks for writing them. Best of luck."

"You too." Oddly enough, Spence said nothing to her. Just waved. We boarded, and he put his carry-on in the overhead bin, taking the window seat per usual. I had to be on the aisle. I tucked my laptop under my seat.

"Okay," he said after we'd buckled up, "that was kinda weird."

"What?"

"What happened back there at the gate. I just...I don't know. I can't explain it."

"You don't *have* to explain it," I said. "Not to me, anyway. Grief is a weird emotion. We all deal with it differently."

We looked at each other for a moment, and I lost myself in his blue eyes and his adorably chipped tooth as I always did. I knew every line, wrinkle, and freckle on the face staring back at me. I'd seen it nearly every day for over fifty years, and it never failed to move me no matter how much it changed. Or didn't.

And then suddenly, without warning, he kissed me on the forehead. "I love you."

"Backatcha."

He settled back in his seat, leaned his head on the window, and was asleep before everyone else finished boarding.

No matter how many times or from what direction we approached, I was always startled to see a gate stretching across the road up the mountain. I was accustomed to the dirt road it used to be, marked only by a black, wrought iron mailbox on a spindly post and a narrow path through the trees. Spence stopped the rental car, punched in the code, and we waited for it to open.

The sign that denoted *The Grove* was the sort of tasteful that denoted wealth, as were the ten lanes branching off the road. Staggered right and left were Aspen, Birch, Cottonwood, Dogwood, Eucalyptus, Fir, Ginkgo, Hawthorne, Ironwood, and Juniper. Each lane had three driveways with a house to the north, one to the south, and a third at the terminus of the lane. There were thirty homes in all—some of the most prime real estate in the county. Prices were subject to fluctuation, but one on Juniper went for 1.75 million when we were there in February.

Beyond that was the old washboardy dirt road for a mile. Nobody got past the development without Miss Lee knowing, at least partially due to the weight sensors at the end of the pavement that rang an alarm. Plus, she'd had so many security cameras installed, she'd had to have a room built off the pantry just for the monitors. Nevertheless, she sometimes had unexpected visitors. And when that happened, they'd find her in her rocker on the porch wearing her flannel shirt and jeans, drinking a nice cup of chamomile tea with her rifle by her side.

"It always breaks my heart to see this development," I said as we passed Juniper and hit the washboard.

Spence slowed the car down. "Me too, but it's kept Riley House open for twenty-five years now. That has to count for something—hey, did you get the email about Berkowitz retiring?"

"Yeah. We should plan something. Maybe take him and Asa out to dinner." My phone rang. "Hello?" I said.

"Are you out of your *mind?*"

"And a good morning to you too, Sidney."

"No, no—a good morning would be me closing your book with a satisfied sigh as I reach for my third cup of coffee, not one in which you kill off your fucking meal ticket."

"*Your* fucking meal ticket, Sidney. Not mine."

"Same diff. Look, you can bring him back, right?"

"I don't think so. They've already had the funeral. I'm not a religious writer—I don't do resurrections."

"Fun-*ny*," he said. "Let's see if you can resurrect the movie deal I'm trying to put together."

"Sidney, you've been trying to put a movie deal together for five years now. No offense, but it's not gonna happen. And I'm okay with that. You're a great print agent. You get me top dollar from the publishers, and don't think I'm not grateful. But Hollywood isn't Doubleday. And I'm tired of writing 'Nathan. I want to do something else."

"Like what?"

"I don't know yet—I just *gave* you a goddamn book."

He turned soothing, but it didn't work. "Let's have lunch today and talk."

"Can't. I'm not in town. My grandmother died last night, so I'm in Colorado."

The line was silent a moment. At least he had *some* respect. "I'm sorry to hear about that, Kent. Really. I know how important she was to you. Are you guys doing okay?"

"Exhausted from being awakened in the middle of the night for a plane trip and really not in the mood to discuss career moves right now, no matter how big a mistake you think they are. I'll call you when I get back." I hung up.

"Let me guess. Sidney finished the manuscript."

"And he's just as delighted as I thought he'd be," I said as we crested the last rise and the big house came into view along with the little house where Chris lived and the circular driveway between them. A rental car was parked in back of Chris's Honda Civic. "Who else is here?" I said. "Surely that can't be Kevin and Roddy already."

But Roddy came out of the house, waving as he popped the trunk open and retrieved a couple of suitcases. He put them down, closed the trunk, and walked over to us as we parked behind him. "*Hola*," he said, running a hand through his greying hair. "Wish we could be meeting under happier circumstances."

"Me too," I replied, getting out of the car and hugging him as Spence got the bags out of the backseat. "How did you beat us here?"

"We live closer. Only spent a couple of hours in the plane. Hey man," he said to Spence, embracing him.

"How you doin'?"

"Never better. How's the architecting?"

"Y'know—a building here, a building there. Pays the bills. You still working for Kevin?"

"Somebody has to keep the books while he's off opening restaurants. How's the writing going, boss?" he said to me.

"Good. Just turned a book in to my agent. Last 'Nathan book."

"The *last*? Why?"

"Getting tired of it. I want to write something else."

"Oh man, that's a shame. We love those, but you gotta do what makes you happy," Roddy said, picking up his bags. I started to do the same, but Roddy put a hand out. "I think Chris has you set up in the big house."

"Oh—but you guys are staying here with Chris?"

"Yeah. Only two bedrooms out here."

"Right," Spence said, grabbing the suitcases. "I'll just take these up to our old room in the big house."

I didn't get a chance to ask him if he felt as weird and excluded as I did. I tried to brush it off. "How's Chris doing?"

Roddy seesawed his hand in the air. "He's trying to keep it together, but you can tell he's hurting. I'm glad you guys are here for him."

Well, we're over *there* for him, I thought. "Can I go in and see him?" I asked, as if I needed permission.

"Yeah, yeah, sure." Roddy started up the walk, and I followed. He veered off toward the guest bedroom—the third one had long ago been turned into Chris's photography/art studio—and I headed for the kitchen, where I heard Chris and Kevin talking.

We had been in college when Jake, Chris's dad, was having the torrid affair with Suey that the whole town was talking about according to Miss Lee, but it didn't last long enough for me to actually meet him. But Jake must have been a stunner if Chris was any indication.

He sat with Kevin at the kitchen table. His eyes were a deep green and exuded the curiosity that made him such a good photographer. He had dark brown hair, and he was clean shaven, but his beard was heavy and the fur of his chest stuck out the neck of his paint-spattered t-shirt. He was trim and muscular, holding his coffee mug with grace and an air of casual masculinity I would have killed to possess. Regardless of whether you were wired for men or women, it drew you in immediately. Everything about him spoke of honesty and trustworthiness.

Kevin had grown into his looks. I always remembered a lanky teenager with untamable hair and a cocksure attitude, all ears and teeth. But age had softened the edges and brought them all into line with each other. His sandy blond hair was well-trimmed even if a little greyer than it had been, and his laugh lines were as pronounced as you'd expect from someone who loved what he did for a living.

"There is too much handsomeness at this kitchen table," I said as I walked in.

They both stood up, Kevin hanging back while Chris stepped around the table and embraced me. I'd be lying if I didn't say I loved the way he smelled faintly of clean sweat and soap. He said something, but the gentle sob escaping him at the same time kept me from understanding it. The words, however, meant less than my reaction. I let him cry into my shoulder, alternately patting and rubbing his strong back until he finished.

He finally stopped, holding me at arm's length, then hugging me again before he picked up his coffee mug for a refill. "Sorry about that," he said. "I'm glad you guys are here. Same crew Miss Lee had here for her birthday. She'd have liked that. She talked about what a great time she had for days after y'all left."

"Same here," I said as Spence walked in. They repeated the scene in the airport, only less awkwardly.

Still sniffling, Chris refilled his coffee as Roddy came back.

"All unpacked," Roddy said, squeezing Kevin from behind.

Kevin gave him a thumbs up. "Good to see you guys," he said.

"You don't mind me putting you up in the big house, do

you?" Chris asked. "I mean, it's gonna be yours so you might as well get reacquainted with it."

I *did* mind, but now wasn't the time or place or audience to say anything. I decided to take his reasoning at face value. "It's fine," I said, but from the way Spence looked at me, I knew he could tell otherwise.

"I need to cook something," Kevin said.

"Cook something?" Chris said.

Roddy waved his hand in the air. "It's just how he deals with things."

Kevin got up from the table and began rummaging through the fridge. "I mean, we gotta eat, right? Is that all you got in here? Three eggs, a hunk of Swiss cheese, and some scuzzy lookin' pickles?"

"Peanut butter and canned corn in the cupboard. What can I tell you? I don't cook."

"I'll bet Miss Lee has enough to cobble dinner together."

Chris clucked his tongue. "Not really. The last time she cooked was when you guys came down in February. We've been getting pizzas or chicken take out from Meecham's. That's kinda how I knew she was failing."

"Okay," Kevin said, "tell you what. Roddy and I will go down to Safeway and get some sausage, peppers, and pasta and I'll put together something I've been thinking about for the restaurant. Maybe a nice red to go with it. Be right back—no one's gone veg since February, right?"

We all shook our heads.

"You might as well take it over to the big house and cook it there," Chris said. "Miss Lee has more pots and pans and utensils and stuff than I do."

"Good idea."

"And Spence and I can get the dining room ready. I don't imagine you guys used it much for takeout."

"Nah. We ate in the TV room."

"Okay, we're outta here. Be right back."

No sooner did Kevin and Roddy leave than we saw out the kitchen window a pickup coming up the drive, halting in front of the big house. A skinny, yet muscular twenty-something boy in jeans, a dingy white A-shirt, and scuffed work boots got out and headed for Chris's door. His head was down, but he wiped his eyes and coughed once, looking up at the big house with an expression I couldn't quite read.

"Who's that?" Spence asked.

"That'll be Paulie, the guy Miss Lee pays to take care of the place and walk the fence once a week and make sure nobody from the development tears it down—y'know, hikers and such. She had signs posted, but you know how she was about her privacy."

"Well," Spence said. "If it's not too crass considering what brought us out here, I have to say he's an uncommonly good-looking young man." Spence had always been partial to scruffy blonds.

"He drinks too much beer and farts in his sleep," Chris said, looking at both of our raised eyebrows as Paulie knocked. "Don't ask." He opened the door. "'Sup, dude?"

"Not much. Sorry to hear about Miss Lee."

"News gets around fast," Chris said.

"Y'know how Coyote is—people ain't got nothin' to do but

talk. Today'd be the day I start walkin' the fence line. You still want me to do that?"

"Ain't up to me," Chris said. "These are the new owners of the big house and most of the mountain. Uncle Kent, Uncle Spence—this is Paulie Ledbetter."

"Pleased to meetcha." He extended a surprisingly clean hand, which we both shook. "Miss Lee used to call me her security chief," he said with a small smile. "Gonna miss her. So, you still want me to take care of the place?"

Spence and I looked at each other. "Sure," I said. "We haven't decided anything or made any plans yet, so just carry on until you hear otherwise. You come around every Monday?"

"Yessir. It's payday."

"Oh yeah, that's right," Chris said. "Lemme get that for ya." He walked back into the kitchen, and I heard him open a drawer. I just knew it was stuffed with money like Miss Lee used to do. Probably still did.

Paulie looked around awkwardly. "So, I hear talk about some kinda memorial service to y'know, honor Miss Lee. She's done a lot for Coyote."

If there's one thing Miss Lee *wouldn't* have wanted, it would have been a memorial service. Such a tribute would constitute "a fuss," and not be within the scope of her wishes according to either what we knew about her or her last will and testament—which expressly forbade it. But how do you explain that to a whole town?

I tried to hedge as best I could. "Well…the thing is…"

"Here ya go," Chris said, coming back with a fistful of twenties he handed to Paulie. "Three hundred, right?"

"Yep—unless y'all want to give me a raise. Just kiddin'. This is cool. Didja hear what I said about the memorial?"

"Memorial—what memorial?"

"For Miss Lee," Paulie said. "We were kinda hopin' you guys would come."

"Can't," Chris replied. "It's in the will. No memorial services. All she wanted was to have her ashes scattered out at the bridge over the creek where she scattered Mister Lee's right after it was built."

Paulie frowned. "We gotta do *somethin'*," he said. "The reverend says it's disrespectful if we don't."

"Okay, let me put it this way—which is more disrespectful? Having nothing the way she wanted or having something she didn't want?"

The boy looked back and forth between us so quickly, I thought his head might explode. "Why didn't she want nothin'?"

"You know how she was. She hated attention, and a memorial service is definitely attention. Let's just leave it be."

"Okay, but you can't stop people from goin' to Meecham's or whatever to remember her, y'know."

"No, we can't."

Paulie seemed confused. "I guess that's what I'll tell the reverend, then." He stuck his hand out at us again, and we shook. "Thanks for keepin' me on. If I find anything that needs fixin', I'll let ya know. See ya, Chris. Nice to meet you guys." He walked off to his pickup and drove away waving.

Chris waved in response. "Sorry I took over," he said to us. "And I didn't mean to speak for you, either. I mean, I guess you can go if you want to, but it's not something she wanted."

"No, no," I said. "We're totally with you, aren't we?"

"Yep," Spence agreed. "She'd have hated it. She didn't mind doing stuff for people, but she always liked to keep it quiet."

"I just didn't know how to say it to Paulie," I said.

"You gotta be direct."

Spence grinned. "You sound pretty savvy. You must be a local."

"Don't worry," Chris said, returning his grin. "You'll pick it up again in no time"

Miss Lee's house smelled terrific. The bite of onions and garlic was in the air, undercut by the comforting savor of sausage and sweet peppers. We heard Kevin draining pasta in the kitchen as we wrapped up getting the dining room ready. Miss Lee's housekeeper had been lax with the dusting recently, so we had to do a bit of extra work, but we used the good china and got the fanciest placemats, napkins, and silverware from the sideboard. I had no idea why I wanted to make this an event all of a sudden, but I did.

Spence peered inside a drawer while I put out the water glasses. "The bone napkin rings or the mahogany?"

"Bone." I heard Kevin uttering indistinct orders to Roddy in the kitchen, and it sounded enough like dinnertime at the Mercedes General to put a lump in my throat. Chris was over at the little house as he said he had some darkroom work to do. Deliberately old school, he preferred his Leicas and Hasselblads and downtime in the peace and quiet of the darkroom.

"Wow," Kevin said, coming out of the kitchen with a glass of white wine in his hand. "I'm gonna have to look around for something nicer to serve this in. I was just going to bring it out in the stockpot."

"Are we ready to eat?" Spence said, grabbing his own wine off the sideboard and starting to put the napkins in the rings.

"Just about. Bread's almost done. All I have to do is grate some parm for the sausage and peppers and put some herbs on top. I should probably text Chris and let him know we're close."

I was surprised Kevin had Chris's number, but I didn't say anything. They must have exchanged them at Miss Lee's birthday, I thought, but I couldn't remember them doing so. "I think there's a tureen down in the same cupboard with the stockpot. It's got daisies on it."

"Of course it does," Kevin said as he walked back to the kitchen with his phone out, texting Chris.

"Are we getting out bowls or plates?" Spence asked.

"Big bowls from the sound of it—and small bread plates. Do you think it's weird Kevin has Chris's phone number?"

Spence got the bowls down off the top shelf. "Not really."

"How about the sleeping arrangements? Them over there and us over here."

"There isn't much space over there," he said, putting the bowls down and going back for the bread plates. "I'd think it was weirder if they were over here, but we were over there. Why? Does it bother you?"

"A little, I guess. I don't know."

"Well, let me change the subject then—have you thought any more about what we discussed when we found out Miss

Lee was leaving us the house?"

Ah yes, that. "What do we know about running a bed and breakfast?" I said, putting the bowls and bread plates out.

"What did we know about starting an AIDS hospice? And you said yourself you were tired of the city."

"I *am*," I said. "It's not like it was when we moved there, but I'm not sure I want to come back here, either."

"We don't have to stay. I'd want to be here for the renovation, but after that's done, we can always hire someone to work the place. We could travel or whatever."

"What about Chris?"

"What *about* him? He loves it here, he's got his own business, his own place and enough money to do what he wants with it."

"Maybe he doesn't want to live across the driveway from a bed and breakfast."

"He can build a big brick wall."

"Okay, okay—I get it. I really do. We have to do something with the place instead of tearing it down or leaving it sit, and a bed and breakfast is a good option. I just…can we wait until the will's read at least?"

"Sure. And I get your reluctance, too. I mean, this was our home away from home, but it was yours longer. I don't mean to be pushy."

I hugged him hard, almost feeling tears edge along my eyes. "Thanks."

"C'mon you two," Roddy said, carrying in a bread board with a huge loaf on it. "Enough of that mushy stuff. Time to eat. I'll open the wine."

"Did Kevin find the tureen?"

"Yep. He's not loving the daisies, but the sausage and peppers just about fit, so it's all good."

We heard the front door. "Smells great in here," Chris said as he came through to the dining room. "I'm famished—what's for dinner?"

"New recipe for the restaurant," Roddy said. "I'll let the chef tell you about it. Everybody sit—you know how he loves to make an entrance with the food."

"Wow," Chris said, sitting down. "Fancy. I'm not sure my t-shirt and jeans are right for napkin rings and everything."

"You look great," Roddy replied.

"Order up," Kevin said, bringing the tureen through the door with a flourish. "Most places use sausage and peppers as a sandwich filling, but I decided to put some pasta in and then I thought it'd make an excellent entrée at the restaurant. Course, this is just store-bought sausage. I'll probably make my own. We already do our own pasta." He served us a couple of big scoops each in our bowls, then he put the tureen in the middle of the table and sat down. "Dig in, guys."

I was hungrier than I thought I'd be, then I realized I hadn't had breakfast or lunch and it was going on three o'clock. We all ate silently for a few minutes before remarking how delicious it was. Kevin looked pleased.

"What were you working on, Chris?" I asked.

"Photos for a book I'm doing on long term AIDS survivors. I've done most of the interviews either by phone or in person, including Mr. Fuentes over there."

Roddy smiled. "Twenty-five years and counting," he said.

"Undetectable viral load and healthy as a horse."

"He's a living testament to my cooking," Kevin said.

Ah, so that's why they have each other's phone numbers.

"Actually, I was gonna pitch it to your agent if you don't mind, Uncle Kent."

"I'd be glad to hook you guys up. I think he'd be interested, but he's not exactly happy with me right now."

"How come?"

"I killed off 'Nathan Burgoine in the book I just handed in."

"The detective?" Kevin said. "Damn. I *loved* that series."

"Me too," Roddy agreed. "We have them all. Why'd you get rid of him?"

"I thought an even dozen was a good place to stop," I said. "Besides, I want to move on to something else."

"Like what?" Chris asked.

"I think it's time for the memoir. I've been considering it for a while, but when we came up the mountain and I saw the big house, it just made sense."

"Time to dig out the *Dead Books?*" Spence said.

"I think so."

Chris put down his fork and buttered a piece of bread, taking care that every square centimeter of the bread was buttered. Just like his mother used to. "The *Dead Books?*"

"They're diaries your uncle used to keep," Spence explained. "He'd write in them whenever someone we knew died."

"Sounds kinda morbid."

"Maybe, but a lot of our lives are in those deaths. I stopped around the time I started writing 'Nathan. I found them when we moved out of Mercedes General into the condo. Couldn't think of what do with them except send them to Miss Lee for safekeeping. She said she put them up in the attic."

"Is Riley in there?" Kevin asked.

"Absolutely. So's Armand—all the guys from the house."

"I think you should do it," Roddy said.

"Seconded," Kevin agreed.

"Thirded," Chris said. "And I know just who can play me in the movie."

"Sidney doesn't have the best track record with Hollywood, but I'll see what I can do."

We talked some business, made plans to pick up Miss Lee's ashes in the morning, drop by the lawyer's office to sign some things, then scatter her ashes out by the old bridge where she did the same for Mister Lee before all of us were born.

Kevin stood up. "I'll start clean-up," he said, putting the lid on the tureen. He picked it up and took it into the kitchen.

"I can help," Chris said, taking his plate and mine along with the silverware and following Kevin.

Spence finished his water. "As pissed as Sidney is right now, you really think he'll take Chris on?"

"Yeah. He'll get over it once I tell him about the memoir. You know how he's been bugging me to do that. I'm gonna get some water—you want a refill?"

"Please."

I took his glass and got up, my knees popping. I'm old enough to write a memoir, that's for damn sure, I thought. A sense of calm came over me. I was no longer in flux. I'd announced a new project, ending questions from those most likely to ask them and planting the seeds in my own head. All I needed was a title.

After that, it would start growing on its own.

Quiet resolve in my head, I rounded the corner and got a clear view of the kitchen sink where Kevin was standing with his back to me. And Chris was by his side with an arm around his waist, nuzzling his neck. Kevin was snort-laughing and occasionally nuzzling him back. Neither of them saw me. Shocked, I flattened myself against the wall out of sight. When I dared look again, they were lip locked in a full-on kiss.

I went back to the table and poured a glass of wine instead.

"It's none of our business," Spence said, taking off his shirt.

I spat out the toothpaste and rinsed my mouth, turning out the bathroom light as I tied my sleep pants. "I just hate thinking we raised a homewrecker."

"*We* didn't raise him, and how do you know he's a homewrecker? That's a big assumption. How many couples do we know that have arrangements?" He toed off his sneakers and sat down on the bed to remove his socks.

I got in and drew the covers up to my waist. "So, it doesn't creep you out that our nephew is messing around with one of the most devoted couples we know?"

"Why should it? Maybe they stay devoted by bringing in a third now and then. Maybe it's a phase. Maybe they're having trouble and trying something different. We've been there, or don't you remember Stewart? And maybe they won't make it as far as we have. It's just none of our business." He took off his jeans, folded them, and put them on the overstuffed easy chair in the corner, padding over in his boxers and getting in beside me. He kissed my cheek and snuggled into my side. "But it wouldn't surprise me if you get your explanation tomorrow."

"Why?"

"As quiet as you got? Everyone could tell something was eating you. Didn't you feel that awkward uncomfortableness wafting your way all through dessert and coffee? I almost wish you hadn't told me."

"You could have brought it up."

"You want to know? *You* ask. I'm not butting in."

We were both silent for a minute or two. "No wonder they're over there and we're over here," I said.

He raised up and looked me in the eye. "Not *that* again. Is that what's bothering you? You're not being included? Something is out of your control? Look, we're here for Miss Lee. Chris is going to pick her up from the crematory tomorrow morning, we'll go to the lawyer's, dispose of the ashes, and that'll be it. Then we leave and let them do whatever they want. It's *none* of our *business*." He settled back down again.

He was right. It wasn't any of our business, but these things always wind up with someone getting hurt, and I didn't want that to see that happen. Everyone seems to be an adult here but me. I should just let it go like Spence said. I scrunched down, and he burrowed with me. But even though I closed my eyes, I knew it'd be a long time until I got to sleep.

"Biscuits," he breathed into my ear.

He wasn't wrong. The morning smelled yeasty and slightly buttered, but not in a Southern way. I raised my head and took another long sniff. "Scones."

"Right. Kevin's we-need-to-talk breakfast."

And certainly enough, we heard a quiet, arrhythmic knock but it sounded more like Roddy's than Kevin's. "Guys?" Roddy said softly. "Kevin sent over some scones. Said you'd want them warm not microwaved."

"We'll be right out," I said. We peed, brushed our teeth, threw on the same clothes from the night before and stumbled barefoot out into the dining room, where a mound of freshly baked blueberry scones sat, surrounded by a dish of clotted cream, some orange juice and a couple carafes of coffee. How he'd done all that without waking us up, I don't know.

"What's all this?" Spence said, not letting anything stop him from pouring coffee.

"Continental breakfast for the new owners," Roddy said. "Sit. Eat. Listen to the apology before you judge."

"Apology?" I said as we all sat down.

"We should have told you. I got outvoted." He buttered a scone, careful to get every corner of the piece. He must have picked that up from Kevin, who picked it up from Chris.

I stirred a spoonful of sugar into my coffee. "Told us what?"

"Oh, come *on*, papi. You saw Kevin and Chris in the kitchen 'doing dishes,' didn't you? It's okay. I know all about it. I think it's kinda cute—in a weird sort of way."

"I told you it was something like that," Spence said, putting a warm scone and a dollop of cream on his plate.

"I *know*," I said with a sigh, "but why Chris?"

"Beats me," Roddy said. "But the second they met out here at Miss Lee's birthday, all Kev could do was talk about him. I finally told him to go for it, and they had some wild weekend in Denver together, and then Kev came home. They make each other happy, and that makes *us* happy—Kevin and me, that is. Hey, we've been together almost thirty years. We were so young when we met. I'm sure you guys get it."

I broke a scone in half and took a bite. "We do."

"Yeah, but you guys are both HIV negative still, right?"

"Right."

"See, there's always been that barrier between me and Kevin. Physically, psychologically. You might think living with it for thirty years makes a difference—and it *does*—but you always wonder. Are we safe enough? Did the condom break? Leak? Back for tests. Any kind of passion has to be tempered. Sometimes the precautions aren't worth the trouble. It's frustrating. You adjust because you have to, but it gets old. Kevin gets something from Chris that I can't give him, and I love him enough to make sure he gets it."

"I just feel responsible."

"For what?" Spence said. "Two entirely independent human beings over the age of twenty-one? Not *everything* is your fault, Kent."

"For real," added Roddy.

I was trying to formulate a response when the phone both rang and chimed. A call *and* a text. I scooped up the phone, letting it ring once more as I glanced at the text. It was from Chris.

Don't call the police!! Will explain.

Startled, I picked up the call. "Hello?"

"Kent? This is Earl down at Robison's Funeral Home. I don't know how to tell you this, but someone just stole Miss Lee's ashes."

Gnats and mosquitos flitting around my face, I heard the swish of the oncoming branch and blocked it with my forearm. I'd seen too many Three Stooges shorts to fall for that one. Chris's back nearly disappeared as he strode through some particularly dense underbrush, but I stayed with him. "Tell me again why we're not going to the police," I said.

He stopped and looked back at me with the same surety I'd seen in his mother's face so often. "Paulie doesn't *need* the police. He just needs a little talking to, so we're just gonna walk up nice and friendly to his cabin and do that. Besides, I can't think of any situation those good ole boys would be able to improve on around here."

"But why would he take her ashes?"

He slapped at a mosquito on his neck. "Because he doesn't think we're going to do right by her. He wants a whole memorial service."

"But *why?*"

His certainty turned to something else as his posture changed. He looked over at the trees on the right, staring a bit before he turned back to me. "So, did Miss Lee's lawyer tell you about the change in her will? The one from last week?"

"He left a message for me, but I forgot to get back to him until you just said something. Why? Is there a problem?"

"Not really, I guess. She's leavin' Paulie some cash—about 250 grand."

"So? She's probably grateful to him for looking after the property and decided to set him up. That's just like her. Unless you think he coerced her somehow."

"Coerce Miss Lee? You must be jokin'—watch out for the creek here." He negotiated the three-stone path I'd forgotten about with ease, the center one a bit taller and wider than the others, waiting for me on the other side. As always, I misjudged the distance on the last one and ended up with my shoe in the muck.

"Shit," I said, leaning on the usual tree trunk to wipe it off.

Chris turned away, but I still saw him smirk as he sat down on a stump. "I think I know why she left him the big bucks," he said, looking at me with deliberateness. "But you're not gonna like it."

I held on to the trunk with one hand and scraped my foot against the brush. "It's not mine to like or not. It's what she wanted to do, though this sounds like something we ought to know about."

"Yeah. Well, they were…um…involved. Romantically."

I lost my balance for a moment. "*Romantically?* She was a hundred years old, Chris. I mean, literally a hundred years old. He's…what, twenty-six?"

"Yep. Same age as me."

"You must be mistaken," I said, taking a few squishy, tentative steps to the stump and sitting down beside him. "Either that or Paulie is a lot more savvy than I thought."

"See, that's just it," he replied, stretching out his long legs.

"I've known him ever since junior high school, and there's not a disingenuous bone in his whole body. He can't lie or hide his feelings—it's just not in him—so for him to take her ashes really says something. And I know there's something going on because I saw them."

"You saw them where? Doing what?"

"Just outside the back door of the big house where the trail we're on starts. They were in a clinch, lost in a kiss. He had his hand on her ass."

"Why did you have to give me that visual? I don't even want to *think* about it."

He chuckled. "I know, right? Look, I thought the same thing when I saw them, but then I figured they were both lonely for something. They recognized it in each other and took some risks to find a little happiness however it looked. As long as it's genuine—and I think this was—how can you fault that? Same thing with me and Kevin."

"Ah yes. You and Kevin."

"Judgy tone, dude." He tucked his legs in and leaned forward, putting his elbows on his knees and looking back at me. He brushed a lock of brown hair out of his eyes. "Don't take this the wrong way, Uncle Kent, but maybe you've been with Uncle Spence so long you don't remember what it's like to be alone."

Alone. Had I ever really been alone? I went from being Suey's little boy doll to Spence's companion and never looked back, and I can't recall a time I was either alone or lonely. My good fortune and privilege suddenly rose up, flushing my face with hot embarrassment. There had to be a word for that. Probably in German. *Schwetzenkerfuffle.*

When the fuck did I get so provincial and narrow-minded? I wondered. We know lots of guys in triads and even more complicated arrangements. Okay, I'm not *related* to any of them, but the principle is the same. Miss Lee and Paulie? With Miss Lee, it sort of makes sense—independent woman who lives life on her own terms has a thing for younger guys, blah blah blah, but from Paulie's end? I don't get it, but then again, I don't *have* to. All I have to do is take it as seriously as they do.

"Okay, now you're all pissed off, right?" Chris said, getting up from the stump.

"No. I understand what you mean, and I need to think about it. I've gotten smug. But right now, we need to be getting Miss Lee's ashes back before hotter heads back home call the cops. The clearing is just ahead if I remember right." I stood up and peered through the trees.

"Yeah, but it's a lot bigger now and has a big-ass cabin Paulie built in the middle."

"By himself?"

"Pretty much. I helped with the concrete work and some of the framing, but he did the rest. That was a great summer."

"Is that when you found out he drinks too much beer and farts in his sleep?"

He looked at me sharply, then half-grinned. "Yeah, it was. Couldn't last, though. Once the cabin was up, we were over. We're kinda different. You ready to go get this done?"

"Yeah," I said as he turned and started off. "So, he must be bisexual or something?"

"Dude, the *labels*. Maybe it's ju—" A sharp crack came from up ahead and the tree ahead of us exploded, raining bark and bits of wood down on us. I instinctively stopped and ducked down, but Chris kept walking—headed for the clearing as he spoke.

"Paulie, what the *fuck?* You tryin' to put somebody's eye out with that goddamn thing? Put it down *now* before I come in there and cram it up your ass."

In response came another explosion from above, but it didn't slow Chris down. I watched him ahead of me as he brushed aside the last few branches and disappeared from my view, stepping into the clearing. I crept up behind him and peered between some bushes.

"Ain't scared," Chris said, crossing his arms over his chest. "If you really wanted to take us out, you coulda done it before we crossed the creek. Put the goddamn rifle down and stop wasting ammo. You can't afford it. But, hey, maybe you can after all."

The gun barrel disappeared from the window beside the door, which was jerked open from the inside. Paulie stood in the doorway, the rifle pointed at Chris. "I didn't want any money. I told her, but she went ahead and did it anyways. The lawyer dude told me last night over the phone. I ain't even slept." His eyes were red and his nose runny as if he'd been crying.

"She wanted you to have it, man. You know how she always liked to take care of people. She knew she couldn't stick around forever, so she took care of us all the only way she could. Ain't nothin' to point a gun at anyone for."

Paulie wavered, softening his stance a bit and letting the rifle fall slack before he re-shouldered it, his rage renewed. "What do you care? You weren't gonna do a goddamn thing for her now she's gone. Not fuck all. She deserves better than that."

Edging forward, Chris raised his hands. "Wait," he said. "Let's back up to our last conversation, dude. That's not what I said. We're gonna scatter her ashes and remember her as a family. And I'm thinking the reverend didn't have anything to do with any memorial service in town. It was all you, right?"

"They didn't know her like I did. *Nobody* knew her like I did."

"That's fair, that's fair. Look, I know about you guys. I saw you on the trail late one night. So, I feel shitty I didn't recognize that, okay? How about you help us scatter Miss Lee's ashes like she wanted? It's only right. You're family, after all. We got it. It's all good."

By this time, Chris was about a foot away from the doorway, close enough to grab the gun. But he didn't have to. At the word *family*, Paulie melted like butter in the hot sun, barely taking the time to prop the rifle against the door jamb before he collapsed sobbing into Chris's arms. Chris wrapped him in his arms and let him cry it out, rubbing his back or shoulders as Paulie clung to him and wept.

Again, I felt a slight pang of jealousy, wondering why I wasn't capable of that while at the same time being glad I wasn't. And after a few moments, I just began to get uncomfortable watching their grief play out while I squatted in the bushes. Nor could I think of a smooth entrance, so I ended up turning around and going back to the big house. Before I negotiated the creek again, I texted Chris in case disaster happened and I fell in with my phone.

I'll leave you guys to work it out. See you at the big house.

I regretted wearing the tie the second we walked out the back door of the big house. I didn't see the point of dressing up to walk a quarter of a mile to scatter Miss Lee's ashes. After all, it was just family. Maybe I'd seen so much death, I assumed I had a more casual relationship with it—one that didn't involve buttoned up collars and shoes that pinch. But I was in the minority. Thankfully, I was able to find something in our rather deep closet.

I thought we'd also need to outfit Paulie, but he turned up in a very handsome navy-blue blazer and slacks with a white shirt and red tie. "Miss Lee got me this a while back in case she wanted me to take her somewhere nice," he said. "Well, nicer'n the footbridge across the creek anyway." He started to tear up again.

We covered the half mile in couples. Spence and I led, Paulie and Roddy behind us with Chris and Kevin bringing up the rear. I was carrying the box with Miss Lee's ashes. So many times we've done this, I thought. So many people. All different in life but the same dust at the end.

"Is somebody gonna say something?" Paulie asked Roddy. "On the bridge, I mean? About Miss Lee? This is the first time I ever done this, and I don't wanna look stupid."

"You can say something if you want to," Roddy said, putting his arm around Paulie's shoulders and drawing him in a bit, "but you don't have to. Some people can't say a word, and you can't shut some up. It depends. As long as what you say or what you don't say is from a place of love, it's the right thing."

I smiled at his advice. He was usually the one to say a kind word during informal ceremonies like this and never left the scene without comforting someone. But how familiar do you have to be with this whole process to begin to identify mourning patterns? Spence will get very quiet, sometimes even looking like he's thinking hard about something before he opens his hand and lets them fall. I've always wondered what he thinks about, but I've never asked him. Maybe it's different every time. I don't need to know anyway.

Kevin will say "Godspeed" as he lets his portion go, even though that's the only time he ever lets the word "God" pass his lips. I've always been curious as to how he came to that expression and why this is the only context in which he uses it. Roddy will mutter a soft prayer in Spanish—the only time I've ever heard him utter a prayer in any language.

Our footsteps rang out on the tiny bridge, the noise backed by the burble of the creek beneath. I went just beyond the middle, turning and leaning on the left rail before I signaled everyone to gather around. I apportioned out her remains, Paulie hesitating only a second before taking his share from the box. I gave Spence his and kept the box. "Check the wind before you let her go," I reminded everyone.

"Godspeed," Kevin said, smoothly tossing ash and bone fragments into the air. He was usually the first, too.

Soft muttering from Roddy, and his share was gone.

Spence leaned over the left rail, frowning in contemplation for a moment or two before he also let Miss Lee fall into the creek and scatter on the breeze.

Paulie dug into the pocket of his slacks and pulled out a film canister, scooping a bit into it. "I'm gonna put this in a locket," he said. He sniffled twice, bellied up to the rail, and sent Miss Lee on her way with a sob and a little smile. "Another death, another path."

I tore my eyes away from the cloud of cremains floating on the air and looked at him. "What did you say?"

He continued smiling, but not at me. "Nothin'. Just…I heard her say it once when she was talkin' about Mister Lee."

Me? I simply let her go. I truly can't remember if that was typical for me or not. But something very atypical did happen. After I turned the box over, the last of Miss Lee spiraling toward the clear running water, a tear welled up at the corner of my left eye. The entire product—the sum of my grief. One tear. I felt it trickle down my cheek, not wanting to wipe it away. If that was to be all, I'd savor it.

"Are you crying?" Spence asked with a hint of incredulity.

His words prompted a second tear dropping down the track of the first. That was all. I brought my hand to my face and wiped it dry, knowing there would not be a third. I breathed a deep sigh and embraced Spence. Kevin signaled to me over Spence's shoulder.

"Let's go eat," he said. "I've got leftover sausage and peppers along with a nice salad, some fresh baguettes, and a couple bottles of wine. We'll make some toasts and tell some stories. Like we used to."

Like we apparently still do. "You guys go ahead," I said. "We'll be right there."

He and Chris walked slowly back to the big house, holding hands. Paulie and Roddy followed them. Paulie looked a bit shaken, but Roddy had an arm around his waist and was whispering into Paulie's ear. He'd be fine. They'd be fine. We'd be fine.

"You ready?" Spence asked, unfolding himself from me.

"Yeah. I could eat. It's been a long morning."

I took his hand, and we sauntered along behind Roddy and Paulie, who had their heads very close together. Spence nodded toward them. We looked at each other, raised our eyebrows, and started chuckling. "Who knows?" I said. "Stranger things have happened. So, how many guest rooms you think we can get out of the big house?"

"Really?" he said, the look of excitement in his eyes far outweighing any possible objection I could have. "You want to do this?"

"Why not? I think I'm finished living in the city. We can make this place ours. Open it up. Redecorate. If we hate it, we can always hire someone to manage it and do something else. But I want to stay here long enough to finish *The Dead Book* at least."

"*The Dead Book?* Is that the title?"

"I can't think of what else I'd call it. But before I even start getting the journals down, I have to ask if this is okay with you. Writing about us, I mean. Because I wouldn't be writing about just me. I couldn't. That means revisiting some pretty ugly stuff. You really sure you want to go through it? Because if you're not, I'll drop it and do something else."

Roddy was now massaging the back of Paulie's neck with one hand, and I smiled to myself. He'd worked fast with Kevin, too.

"This is important to you."

I shrugged. "Not as important to me as you are. I'll always get another idea."

He copied my shrug as we reached the back door. The others went inside, but we hung back a bit.

"I'll be okay," he said. "I lived through it once, I can live through it again. Remember our deal. You take care of the stories, and I'll take care of the buildings. It's worked out pretty well so far, and I want this story out there."

"Be careful what you wish for."

"That's how I got you."

"Nah," I said. "It was your fringe."

He grinned, showing off the chipped tooth that won my heart. "Ah, that leather jacket—I thought I was John fucking Lennon back then. Whatever happened to that, anyway?"

"It's probably up in the attic."

Kevin popped the door open, standing there with a bottle of wine in each hand. "White or red?" We didn't answer quickly enough. "Never mind, I'll open both. Hurry up, you two." He closed the door again.

"Another death, another path," I said, more rolling the phrase around in my head than anything else.

"I saw your eyes light up when he said that," Spence said. "That's going to be a chapter title, isn't it?"

"Maybe," I replied. "Maybe."

FIN

ABOUT THE AUTHOR

Jerry L. Wheeler is the editor of seven anthologies of gay erotica for Bold Strokes Books, Wilde City Press, and other publishers. His own collection of short fiction and essays, *Strawberries and Other Erotic Fruits* was shortlisted for the Lambda Literary Award in 2012. His first novel, *Pangs*, was released by Queer Space/Rebel Satori Press in 2022. He lives and writes in Denver CO, maintaining his review blog, *Out In Print: Queer Book Reviews* (https://outinprintblog.wordpress.com/) and his own editing business, *Write And Shine* (https://jerrywheelerblog.wordpress.com/). He promises never to mention *The Dead Book* again.

Printed in the USA
CPSIA information can be obtained
at www.ICGtesting.com
JSHW021942230324
59709JS00003BA/168